Gavin is an ordinary young
clearance estate development
Although a challenge for his parents, an underachiever at school and socially unacceptable to his peers, he nonetheless carries his own personal mystery and through him we experience a fascinating perspective into a uniquely rich world which gradually takes on a whole life of its own. This disturbing and starkly honest novel makes no attempt to get inside Gavin's head but traces his troubled life through a series of closely-observed episodes and gritty adventures that lead to the mordant climax of his adolescent destiny.

"This is an extraordinary and enlightening book, and especially so for having been written by an eighteen-year-old. Wonderfully descriptive and evocative of the physical, emotional and spiritual poverty of a housing estate in the North-East in the early 1960s, the story shows how tragically and easily under-privileged children can slip through the cracks and deteriorate during the years in which they should be flourishing. Thorley's perception of human nature is deep and penetrating, and this book could rightly take its place on courses in sociology, education and psychology, as well as being a very good novel in its own right."

Lara Owen, author of *Her Blood Is Gold* and *Growing Your Inner Light*.

"I am shattered. When I read this it is like I am watching a film; it is very emotionally immediate. I am overcome by your powers of observation. Because you make his experiences so real, I live that little boy's life and he is still with me. Your writing is deeply beautiful in a painful sort of way. What a clever young thing you were! Way, way above average!"

Chrissy Philp, author of *One Way of Looking at Man* and *The Golden City*.

"This remarkable first hand account of growing up on Tyneside in the 50s vividly recalls the inner and outer squalor of that dying industrial era. Unusual and haunting, it is an impressive achievement for an eighteen-year-old. I loved it, especially the dialogue, which expresses both dark humour and the pressure to conform. From 2009, it is like looking back at a past age, but this book makes it all amazingly real again."

Derek A Brown, North-Easterner by adoption and choice

"A subtle and interesting book. I found it gripping from the beginning and couldn't put it down. It is at once an evocation of a time that is past, the 1950s and 60s, and a clever weaving of events that recur and echo each other. The milk monitors and the staff room at school, and the coal miners, and the enduring sameness of the human race from the Bronze Age to the future. The same bullies, sex-driven adolescents, husbands and wives who don't understand each other, fire-fighters confronting the public fascinated by disaster, the tricked law enforcement officers – in this marvellous book, all are there. Beautifully written, it is a meticulous observation of the human condition occasionally jewelled by soaring descriptions of nature, as though pointing out that human nature is capable of great beauty – as well as bewilderment and cruelty. It's so moving that the last chapter was almost too painful to read."

Moyra Caldecott, author of *Etheldreda*, *Guardians of the Tall Stones* and *Akhenaten: Son of the Sun*

"*Well Below Average* is one of the few works of fiction I picked up and couldn't put down until I'd read it cover to cover. Thorley's narrative had me immediately engulfed in Gavin's world, with vivid descriptions of the stark reality of lower class Britain in the 1950s. Reminiscent of the compelling observational style of the realist film director Ken Loach, this is a truly fascinating glimpse into the bleak yet subtly rich world of disadvantaged young people."

Sivan Bar-Sever, registered midwife, mother, film buff and self-taught photographer

# Well Below Average

Anthony Thorley

ARCHIVE
publishing

For full details of all our books please visit our website

archivepublishing.co.uk
and
transpersonalbooks.com


This edition published in Great Britain by
**Archive Publishing**
Dorset, England


© Anthony Thorley 2005, 2009

The rights of Anthony Philip Thorley as author have been asserted
in accordance with the Copyrights, Designs and Patents Act 1988.


A CIP Record for this book is available from
The British Cataloguing in Publication data office


ISBN 978-1-906289-16-4 (Paperback)

First published in 2005

Designed at Archive Publishing by Ian Thorp

Cover illustration from a 1976 limited edition print of slum clearance
entitled *Newcastle upon Tyne* by Norman Wade.

Printed and bound by Lightning Source

*For Celia*

## AUTHOR'S NOTE

Until the last few weeks, the handwritten manuscript of this novel sat in a box for over forty-two years since it was written by an eighteen-year-old in 1962-63. I still have a vivid recollection of the late night I came back from a friend's house, head buzzing with too much coffee, and found myself through a subsequent sleepless night strangely compelled to write a novel about my experiences growing up in the 1950s on an estate on the northern fringe of Newcastle upon Tyne. I had no literary pretensions or experience and indeed have written nothing fictional since, but the need to express myself at that particular time in my life could not be denied.

It was during what would be now called a gap year between grammar school and entering Cambridge to read medicine, in order to pursue a long career in psychiatry, that I was faced with the strangely contrasting opportunity of either spending six months working with Inuit in Greenland or teaching in a secondary modern school in Gateshead. I chose Gateshead with no sense of pretentiousness, as I was aware that my future as a doctor would very likely forever take me away from the heart of the rich local culture in which I had grown up.

*Well Below Average* and the story of Gavin was the product of this experience and, as I see more clearly now, a kind of closure on my own childhood and adolescence. I felt compelled to try and record some of the raw lives that I had experienced directly and indirectly. As a young man I was very affected by the contrasting social opportunity of my own situation and many of the people I had played and grown up with. The 60s were a time of a much more divisive social meritocracy than I see today, and I was one of the fortunate ones.

The novel came very easily, many of the episodes being completely true in life, so I had little need to plan and set out the basic story. There was one rough draft before the final version, and the whole was finished in about six months. I realised at the time that although I was fascinated by what made people tick and what went on in their minds, and how this externalised in their actions and attitudes, I had virtually no idea what went on in the head of a boy like Gavin. Although both on the streets and in my subsequent teaching experience I had met many forms of Gavin on many occasions, I was perplexed and challenged by the nature and qualities of his inner life. So I purposely made this book primarily observational, describing the environment and the behaviours that I knew so well, but making little comment on the thoughts and inner worlds of any of the characters involved. At the time I had little literary experience and had read few modern novels, but I particularly enjoyed John Steinbeck and the kind of biological observational style he employed through his biologist friend Ed Ricketts in *Cannery Row*, and in describing the disastrous sexual fumblings of Lennie in *Of Mice and Men*. These influences are crudely evident in *Well Below Average*.

I wrote the whole novel in secret, with only my girlfriend of the time and a couple of grammar-school friends who had shared with me the same estate experience actually knowing anything about it. During the writing I showed it to no-one. Then one of my friends read the final version in the summer of 1963, but perhaps mercifully made little comment. I think my enthusiasm and crude outpouring was kindly tolerated by my erudite friend who was to go on and become a distinguished university historian.

Soon after I went to university I told my parents about my writing but they also passed little comment, seeing it as another passing phase and more evidence of my creative eccentricities. With the business of medical studies sweeping me into a new life, I put the novel away and have never returned to it for re-writing or revision.

Reading it again and preparing it for publication has both surprised and pleased me. I am deeply affected by the memories it has brought flooding back, and how accurate they are. I am fascinated by my own pre-psychiatric view of my early experiences and what they seem to reveal about me as a person over the last forty years. To me, it reads more like a blunt personal autobiographic diary of childhood memories rather than a novel with any literary style and flow. However, a number of impressions for me remain indelible. So many of the childhood conversations are clipped, do not develop or become reflective and are relatively bereft of imagery. Behind them there is often a great deal of social posturing, with threats and fear never far away. And now I recall how frightening it actually was. And how, before the universal bicycle, so much of a young boy's life was then spent running around on the streets and in the fields, and how, in the novel, that outdoor roving life-experience certainly comes through.

The account is almost exactly as the completed manuscript. I have touched up the dialect in half a dozen places and introduced a few half-sentences to make things clearer. Otherwise, this is the novel as written by a shy eighteen-year-old middle-class grammar-school boy whose father did not have an allotment, did not work in a factory and was actually a nuclear physicist. This is the unpolished and unique expression of a rather serious young man who realised that although he was in the fascinating world he describes, he was not of it.

As I look back, I also have to acknowledge that the episodes described in *Well Below Average*, coupled with those of a few years later when I lived with aboriginal Amerindians in Brazil's Matto Grosso, were actually the most important and formative experiences in my young life and profoundly shaped the quality of my subsequent work as a doctor and my most basic values as a person.

My wife of many years, Celia Gunn, an author and novelist herself, knew nothing of this novel until I took it out of its box some weeks ago. I am deeply indebted to her for advice and assistance in preparing the manuscript and for her wonderful loving support in this very personal project.

Anthony Thorley
Bath
September 2005

# One

There was a burst of fire from the automatic rifle.

"Got yer!"

"Ner y' didn't! Yer missed!"

Again the small boy levelled the sites of the rifle. His face screwed up in all concentration as he squeezed the trigger. The noise was directed and deafening.

"Ah got yer that time!"

One of the two other boys span round and steadied himself. He screamed a long high scream and a shudder seemed to run across his body. Then he fell to the ground, rolled over, and lay still. His companion had ducked out of the way and continued running down the shaley bank. At the bottom he darted to one side and took cover behind a pile of loose stones. Gradually he edged his legs behind him until he was lying flat on his belly. Then he propped himself up on his elbows and put his eye to the sights of his space gun. Trigger finger moved silently as he opened fire at the figure on the ridge. The atomising rays snaked out and curled round the unsuspecting boy. He began to glow a greenish white colour.

"Got yer!"

The boy on the bank did not move.

"Got yer, Gavin!"

Slowly, the face of the standing figure twisted in agony, his body bent forward and, clutching his stomach with his left hand, he collapsed in a heap. The plastic rifle fell away from him with a dry clatter.

Down and over the field, the light and even breeze had changed. There was a ripple passing across the long grass and a wall of cooler air stepped up the bank and over the three boys. Tiny brown leaves of a stunted bush span hurriedly on their dead stalks and basking flies were lifted effortlessly from the hot shale and carried elsewhere. The straight brown hair of the motionless freedom fighter was stirred and ruffled. He shivered visibly.

Suddenly and without warning, the dead soldier halfway down the bank began counting aloud.

"Thirty-four, thirty-five, thirty-six … forty-two, forty-three, forty-four…."

The boy with the space gun sprang to his feet, scrambled up the loose shale and stood over the motionless body.

"… Forty-seven, forty-eight, forty-nine, fifty!"

The space gun spat immediately and he was sprayed with rays.

The body rolled over. "You can't do that, man! You never gisuh chance!"

"That doesn't matter. At fifty, yer were alive again."

"But you never gisuh chance." He looked up towards the ridge. "Hey, Gavin! Haven't you got to get to cover before yer can be shot out again?"

Gavin stood and picked up his rifle.

The boy with the space gun was suddenly angry. "Ye get down too, Gavin! Ye haven't counted up to fifty yet, either."

"Ah have!" shouted Gavin as he edged down the slope, picking his way around tufts of spiky yellow grass. Overhead, the sun was set in grey cloud and shone pale and watery. "Ye've not got to shout, anyhow!" He continued running up to them.

"Yis yer have!" shouted the boy on the ground.

"Yer haven't," repeated Gavin.

"Yis yer have!" both boys shouted together.

"Who asked ye, John Sims?" Gavin glared at the boy on the ground. "Ah thought ye were shouting for me! Now y're on his side!"

"Ye have to shout, man," replied John Sims, "so that yer can tell when y're alive again!"

"Ye divvn't," said Gavin sullenly.

"Ye dee," answered John Sims, raising his voice.

"Divvn't."

John Sims jumped up and held up his fist in front of Gavin. He had made his face evil and menacing. "Ye dee, son," he said slowly. Gavin raised his rifle but John saw the movement. He twisted his lip and grimaced. "Ye just dare, son."

"Divvn't. Divvn't. Yer divvn't," mumbled Gavin, all low, half frightened, half taunting.

John poked his fist into Gavin's face, but Gavin was too quick and bobbed back a step. He was ready to move again, and he was still muttering. "Divvn't, yer divvn't, yer divvn't." He began shaking his head.

John was becoming more angry. "But ye's got up! Ah didn't get up until now!"

"Aye, but ye've just been shot again."

"Aye, but Ronnie didn't gisuh chance."

"Aw, shurrup!" shouted the boy with the space gun.

"Shurrup yerself!"

"It's always the same when ye's play with anybody, Gavin Cooper. Yer never stick to the rules."

"Ah dee! It's ye who-"

"Yer divvn't," agreed John.

"Well, ye knar what ye's are, Ronnie Walker, divvn't yer?" shouted Gavin a few inches from Ronnie's face.

Both boys moved towards him. Gavin was forced to move back. There was open invitation on their faces. And now John began taunting. "Ye's just dare say! Gan on! Ye's just dare say!"

Gavin fixed his eye on Ronnie, who was a little taller. By now John Sims's contrived face of menace had gone and his breath was coming in little gasps of a true anger. For a moment they all stood there, tight and motionless, each waiting for a move from one of the others.

Gavin tensed himself. "Right, when y're feeling that way...." He paused. "When y're feeling that way, there's only one thing for me, and that's to gan yem." And suddenly he ran around them and down the path.

For a moment they started after him, but he was too far ahead.

"Babee! Babee! Gannin' to yer Mam!" shouted Ronnie.

"Softee! Babee!" cried John. "Geet babee, ye!" He bent down and selected a stone from the shale. He sized the distance, and then he flung it at Gavin as hard as he could.

But Gavin was not looking back and just ran on down into the field. The stone hit some rocks on the path, bounced aside and span into his thigh. He was running so fast that there was no pain or feeling. The path twisted across the field and then followed up a slope so that at the crest he could see the first row of council houses. On his left was the Catholic primary school. Some kids had been playing in the playground; now they were scurrying round by the fencing trying to find a lost ball in the long grass. They were too occupied to notice Gavin slow to a trot on the rise. Now he looked round, but John Sims and Ronnie were not chasing after him. Already they had turned up the embankment towards the row of old coal tracks on the skyline. Gavin started to walk down to the houses. At the corner of Aln Gardens, the Spoleti Brothers ice-cream van was surrounded by a crowd of mothers and little children. The chimes of "Oranges and Lemons" rose up to meet him.

He began trotting through the dry grass and burdock. Hair fell across his eyes and he tossed his head and flicked it aside. The hair slipped down again and he was panting a little. He raised his arm to wipe the hair away, but again the jerk of his head was successful. He licked salt from the back of his wrist.

Gavin was only a small lad, not short and stumpy like that family of fat kids who lived opposite the Co-operative, but slight and, in a way, strangely adequate. It was as if his bones had stopped growing just as soon as they were big enough to do the job they were designed for. The muscles and flesh on his limbs had always enabled him to run far, but not fast. He was tough enough to take knocks and bruises, but a bad fall could send him home, crying in the kitchen. He was strong, but he could easily be held to the ground by bigger lads his age. There was just enough Gavin Cooper to see him through most trials without harm, but there were no special features, there was nothing in excess.

His mother had been married eighteen months when she found herself pregnant. None of the neighbours could ever decide whether she wanted a child or not, and then she fed their curiosity with a strange story about how it had been a miracle anyway with her husband on nights all the time. The pains started just after a cup of tea late one January afternoon. A taxi was ordered. She was rushed to the Queen Elizabeth Hospital. Her labour was short and the birth a model of normality: easy movements; a sure, uncomplicated delivery. But she had not really cared when the nurses held him up, wet-skinned and kicking. Even the midwife remembered that she was the only mother that week who had turned away, face into pillow. Usually the mothers smiled, sometimes from far away, dim and distant far beyond in the fading anaesthetic, but they smiled, and the sweat on their faces became tears. But Mrs Cooper had turned away. She insisted on telling the nurses for the first four days that she had had no baby, and it wasn't until the first week had gone by that she was able to accept him. Mr Cooper had come as soon as their son was born and he stared at the red thing in the cot, and poked his finger through the rails and smiled a little. As his wife got to know the baby she found the yellow skin of his birthmark on his tiny thigh, and complained and threatened the staff that she been given a marked baby.

Gavin was the name they gave to him, but that was much later. Gavin had been Mrs Cooper's brother, until he had walked across a Chinese minefield in North Korea three months before. Mr Cooper thought that his wife would take this news badly, especially when she had placed her brother's photograph on the dresser shelf. But instead, she decided to call the baby by the same name. Then Gavin was nearly six months old. Previous to that his mother always called him simply "the baby", and his father did likewise, although he sometimes referred to him as "the little lad".

It was months later that Mrs Cooper was able to tell her neighbours that she was glad that he'd grown up such a healthy and tough little boy. This made him much less trouble, and the neighbours always agreed. Mr Cooper never heard any of these conversations because he was always in bed all day, and when Gavin made any noise in the house and was running around trying to escape from his mam, Mrs Cooper always cornered him eventually and then made sure that he was silent. That way his dad didn't get wakened up like he used to when Gavin was still a baby, and come down into the kitchen yawning and getting in the way.

Gavin's face was like a thousand others: quite rounded; nose flat; eyes blue; lips, thin like two lines drawn around his mouth; straight brown hair when it was clean, lank and dark when it wasn't. All this was his own, and yet no one ever stopped in the street when he was out at the Self-service with his mam and said, "What a grand little lad that is!" They had seen his pale cheeks and staring eyes a hundred times before.

He was wearing a pair of well-worn jeans and a beige jacket, all covered in grey-red dust where he had fallen on the shale. One of the back pockets was torn and hung from two copper studs. The jacket had fitted someone in a shop long ago, but now it seemed awkward and square on his narrow shoulders. A belt, no longer in contact with his jeans because of his running, gathered a dirty blue shirt to his body. The jeans however were in no danger, and the purpose of the belt became obvious as he tucked in his automatic rifle with a practised skill.

His shoes were dirty and he was panting a little as he left the field and joined the old cinder track, padded flat by generations of miners. Gavin stared at the streaming blur of tiny coke and coal particles. Like some endless belt, they glimmered and sparkled and then stopped abruptly as if someone had switched them off, and were replaced by the white concrete of Cresswell Road.

When he got to the ice-cream man he walked past, turned around, and stared for a long time at the dirty white van. Suddenly he felt in his pocket for a coin that had been pressing into him for days every time he had sat down. He looked at the object in his fingers. It was an old washer, correct in every dimension with a sixpence, but with a hole in the middle. He threw it across the road. His broad face and blue eyes clearly showed his disappointment, and as if to forget the incident he broke into a trot for a few yards, holding his gun Indian-fashion, then slowed and continued walking.

The ice-cream man sounded his crackling shines, revved his engine and moved off down the street. As he passed, Gavin gave him no second look and instead turned into Craster Avenue.

Craster Avenue was just one street in the big estate development which had taken place on the city boundaries. People had been moved from the crumbling rows of houses down by the river, out onto the new estate on the fringe of the countryside. Some had complained. They were worried about losing the old ways. The bus fares would be higher, they said. And what about the old pub down the road? And the little corner shops? People even started to wonder what was going to happen to the big non-conformist chapel, but no one ever went in. After the cranes and bulldozers had been and gone, only the shops and pubs and church remained standing, alone in a sea of rubble, island shadows of the old community. And one by one even they would fall, until only the big Gothic church was left and around its tapering spire a new community would grow up. Flat-dwellers. People who were able to gaze out from their ten-storey balconies and see, far below in the valley, dock-cranes, bridges and power stations. Below them, new shops and playing fields, planned trees and, set on a concrete plinth, a modern sculpture which the town hall people claimed to understand even if no one else did.

It was the old people who were the most difficult. Many felt they would die sooner if they went out to the new estate. They said things would never be the same, and it was too late to change their way of life. But the young people looked at their pale children and remembered the endless soot on the washing, and they were eager to be near the country and the real sun and the new houses.

So they moved their homes, carried away their sticks of furniture and settled on the estate. One by one, the streets and avenues had taken life as they filled up with new people. Many old friends from the riverside met up again, many new friends were made, new gossip was created and a new community slowly emerged. The young people worked hard to pay for instalments on their televisions and washing machines, vacuum sweepers and furniture, and soon many were running small cars and making trips to the sea at weekends. And the old people gazed with tired eyes through the windows at the noisy children outside, and their polished walnut chiming clocks sat on their mantelpieces, ticking quietly.

These kind of people had lived in the avenue for five years now. Many children had already been born who would never know the steep cobbled streets leading to the oily river and the things to be discovered in the bomb-site where the old Co-operative warehouse once stood. Instead, they were children of the building site, playing in the sand heaps and the drainage pools, and hitching lifts from gravel lorries. They watched the other avenues being built and played in the houses, they climbed through the windows and drank the water when it was piped in, and they saw the huge row of white concrete shops grow up overnight.

But soon it was different. Doors became kicked and worn, paint on the windows flaked and chipped, and many wire fences were broken down. Craster Avenue had lost its novelty. Suddenly all the houses were all the same and outside people began complaining about unadventurous planning. They talked of uninspired production line, shoebox dwellings and poor building standards. Letters appeared in the local press and after a while painters and repair-workers were sent in by the Corporation, but it made no difference. This first generation of the new estate had found their equilibrium and there were echoes of the old riverside in almost every street.

As the houses became dulled and worn, the saving feature of the estate became more and more the way in which the gardens were tended. Some were neat and had close-cropped green lawns and clean white paths of concrete. Around the lawns were bright borders of flowers and young bushes reaching deep into the clay soil. Others were very untidy, harbouring long yellow-green grass, sulking weeds and clumps of dandelions enjoying complete freedom, enemies of no man. Here and there, wallflowers poked through the jungle, suggesting some industrious Sunday afternoon of another season. There were old people's gardens, full of wild weeds and couch, hardly penetrated by spotless white paths where only the milkman passed. And children's gardens, with soil trodden to concrete, marbles and lead soldiers glinting in the long flattened grass and mud on the side-paths. And there was one garden quite different, where the dandelions had long since abandoned hope: a vast sea of cement and crazy paving. This was at the house of Gavin's best friend, Dennis.

Gavin pushed open the yellow metal gate and as always it gave a little squeak in the last few inches of its wing. When it clanged shut again he was standing on the steps and had rung the bell.

He stood staring through the hammered glass by the door waiting for the moving blur that meant someone was in. The blur was yellow when it appeared; soon it got bigger and the door opened. It was Dennis's eldest sister, Sheena. Inside, there was dance music.

"Is Dennis coming out?"

Sheena leaned on the open door and turned into the house. "Is our Dennis coming out?"

No reply. Just the blare of a big band playing scored jazz.

"Turn that thing down!" bawled Sheena into the living room.

In the following silence, for the first time that afternoon Gavin noticed a bird singing .

"Who's there?" a voice called.

"Is our Dennis in?"

"No. He's down at his gran's," the voice replied.

"He's down at his gran's," Sheena repeated, looking down at Gavin.

He stood for a moment as if deciding something. "Okay. Thanks."

He turned away down the path as the door clicked shut, squeaked the gate and heard it clang again as he walked over the street. Ten minutes later, he had passed through the new estate, passed the new Methodist chapel on the corner that they were still building and was walking into the old houses on the edge of the city. Soon he was in the long row of his own street.

Time had allowed these terraced houses to develop a dirty brick and with this, a rich personality. They had no gardens, but here and there a few window-boxed plants fought with cigarette ends and abandoned bus tickets for an outdoor life. This street was mature, its growing pains over many decades ago, its future rather insecure, but its past was whole and cherished.

Gavin rapped the knocker of number thirty-two and shouted through the letterbox. "Mam! It's me!"

There was no reply, but he could smell onions from his father's meal. Onions before the factory floor. Then his mother opened the door.

"Ah didn't see yer coming," said Gavin.

"No, Ah was in the front room," replied Mrs Cooper.

He followed his mother down the long gloomy hall into the kitchen.

"Ah'm just going round to Mrs Wilkinson's," she announced, putting on a coat from the pegs by the kitchen door and patting her white blonde hair in the mirror.

For a moment at Gavin surveyed the kitchen table. Then he turned down the hall. "Mam? Are yer...?"

The front door had clicked shut.

The kitchen table was covered in a green spotted oil-cloth,

drawing-pinned round the edge. On the table were two plates, one covered in crumbs. Pieces of fruit-cake lay on the other. Mr Cooper never liked fruit-cake, but Gavin ate almost anything. He grabbed a piece of cake and crammed it into his mouth. Then he craned up to the mantelpiece and, reaching out with searching fingers, slid the sixpence off and pushed it into his pocket. As it was September, there was no fire and the grate at his feet was full of old comic papers, wrinkled flattened cigarettes, food scraps and a fine coating of soot. He zipped his pocket up and went over to the sink and drank the water straight from the tap. Wiping his mouth with his jacket sleeve, he noticed that one hand had now become cleaner, so he then ran both under the cold tap. When all the remaining dirt was rubbed onto the towel, he went into the living room and turned on the television.

As the picture came on, he was slumped in the worn armchair a few feet away. It was the news, and as the newsreader began to give the latest position on a big Welsh steel dispute, Gavin's eyes slowly focused far beyond the screen. An industrial correspondent caught a union official coming down the steps of the union head-quarters. As the wind chopped and buffeted the microphone, the official explained why the union would have to go to arbitration unless the Minister intervened, and Gavin was a thousand miles away. So in fact was the newsreader, but the camera light flashed again and he returned to read of a new uprising in Migala, in Central Africa. There was film of crowds rioting, running down streets and shouting slogans. A wild mob moved towards the cameraman; a flash of spinning faces and sky. Next shot, a tank and armoured car grinding down a shabby street. Above, bullets whined and tore into window shutters. Over on the left, an upturned blazing car and black smoke and, four feet away, Gavin's eyes alight, his face all excited. Then the news was over. Three boring minutes as the next day's weather was declared with the usual qualifying probability, and then with a rolling and heavily orchestrated American folk tune, a shot of a thousand longhorns crossing the plains, weary and tossing their heads. "Chuck Mason and the Night Rustlers" had begun. Gavin was soon enveloped in its shallow intrigue.

He remained staring at the shimmering screen until he realised that the room was being lit by the streetlights and it was quite dark outside. He got up and put the light on, then suddenly changed his mind and switched it off again. He then left the room, and opened the front door. When he was sure it was just ajar, he scampered off down the street.

Round the corner he could smell them a little. Mrs Baker was already returning with hers under her arm. She called to him in her croaking voice. "Hello, Gavin."

Usually Gavin replied, but tonight he felt very hungry indeed and when he heard her, he only ran faster. She turned round and looked after him, shaking her head.

Around the next corner were the bright fluorescent lights of the chip shop. Two older lads were standing outside talking to a young girl. Gavin could not see their faces as they were in silhouette. Now the smell was delicious. He slowed down to get his breath, pushed open the shop door and took his place in the queue. In front of him there was a retired pitman with large rough hands and rounded fingers, as if the lifetime at the pit-face literally had worn them down. The old man ordered two suppers and, taking the vinegar bottle, gave each three or four solid shakes. All around was the crisp aroma of fat, onions and steaming vinegar.

The fish-man slid a new batch of chips into the fat. They met with an angry roar which gradually subsided into a promising sizzle.

The pitman picked up his warm bundle and shuffled out of the shop, his hobnails sounding noisily on the lino-covered wooden floor.

"Yes, Gavin?" said the fish-man's wife.

"Packet of chips, please."

"Six pennyworth?"

"Aye."

She scooped out the chips, chasing them in the deep fat, using the scoop like a landing net. When she was satisfied that the scoop held a six-pennyworth, she transferred them to a greaseproof bag. Underneath, the Daily Sketch began to develop large grey transparent blotches.

Gavin salted and vinegared them as much as he dared without catching the woman's eye. Then he slid his sixpence across the counter.

"Would yer like a bit of batter on it?" asked the fish-man, holding a scoop of fatty steaming surplus of fish batter.

"Ooh aye."

He shook some batter on the chips and Gavin took the opportunity of having another shake with the vinegar.

"What do you say, then?" asked the fish-man's wife.

"Thank you," said Gavin, almost swallowing the words. Clutching his warm packet, he ran from the shop.

"Canny lad, that Gavin Cooper," remarked the fish-man as he ran haddock fillets through a dish of batter.

When Gavin got home, his tummy felt full and a glow of contentment spread out into his limbs. He closed the front door and went into the living room where the screen still danced and flickered. He slumped into the chair again and did not turn the set off until the last news came on.

In the kitchen he sided the few plates, had another drink of water, rubbed smooth lips together and went upstairs to his tiny bedroom at the corner of the house. In a few minutes he had his pyjamas on and the lights switched out, and was settling down to sleep. He counted the distant hospital bell as it sounded through the night, could not decide whether it was eleven or twelve and was fast asleep when his mother put key to the door.

# TWO

Every morning at about a quarter to eleven, the Co-operative milk lorry was to be found somewhere near the Cooper's home, delivering and collecting milk bottles at most of the doorsteps in the street. For many people, the milk lorry was a sign that the morning was wearing on. Some, as though by a reflex, even glanced at and altered their clocks or began a particular morning chore. However, all the people knew that the milk lorry was not to be relied on at weekends. Then it would come at any time, but usually it came late. No one really knew why this was, but one or two had a suspicion that it was all bound up with the private life of the milkman.

On this Saturday morning, the clatter of the crate and clinking of bottles woke Gavin up. Soon he sat up in bed, yawned, rubbed his eyes and looked through the window.

Down below, the swarthy milkboy was returning to the covered red lorry carrying two crates full of empties. On the lorry, another youth lifted the crates and changed the bottles. The man in the cab was reading a coloured magazine, spread on the steering-wheel. Smoke from a cigarette held in stained fingers curled upwards and was sucked out through the top of the window. The shadows of the moving milkboy and the lorry were nearly in line with the gutter. It would soon be midday.

Across the road all the curtains were open and insides of rooms could be dimly seen. Sometimes a curtain flapped a little against an open window. The draught fanned down on Gavin and made him shiver.

His mother's footsteps were on the landing. She whispered harshly: "Hey, Gavin! Hurry and get up! Ah'm not going to shout at you from fear of waking your father."

As the door was still shut, Gavin pulled a face at her. Then he kicked the bedclothes down to the bottom of the bed and lay still. But soon he shivered again and this made him get up. He stood on the small island of carpet and began to drag his jeans on. Then he heard a milk bottle smash.

He ran into the other front bedroom to get a better look through the window, but by the old clothes chest he felt a sudden pain in his foot and fell onto the carpet with short cry. By his leg lay a small tiepin with a bent gold lion crest attached to it. Gavin rubbed his stinging foot and gasped a little. Then he noticed the tiepin. He picked it up and saw the bent lion. Using fingers from both hands, he tried to straighten the crest but the brittle metal cracked and it broke off. He pressed the crest to the silver pin as if trying to re-weld the metals. Then, after looking around the room and listening quite still for a few seconds, he slipped the broken tiepin into his pocket.

The white pool of milk was still settling in the dusty road, but the pieces of glass were all picked up and pitched by the wall. The swarthy youth swung onto the covered lorry and with a roar it crashed into gear and trundled up the street.

Downstairs, his mother was sitting at the table drinking tea. Gavin took a piece of bread and butter and went to the tap for a drink of water. Catching his mother's eye, he reached for a cup, filled it and drank.

A few minutes later by the swings, he found some of the boys from the Craster Avenue gang.

"Howay, Gavin," they called. "Do y'wunna game of cowas and indies?"

"Ah heven't got me gun," replied Gavin.

"It doesn't matter. We're gannin' ter the fields. You can break a branch and use it as a club. You'll have to be an injun."

Gavin ran up to the playground with them and over the main road and into the fields.

When he got home his father was up and outside the house moving the pile of broken glass. Mr Cooper looked up and his grey eyes were almost apologetic. He did not smile. "Hello, son. Your mother said it was best to move it and throw it all in the bin."

"Ah know. Ah saw it happen. Ah saw the milkman."

His father picked up the brush and shovel and led him into the house. Dinner was nearly ready. The smell of roast lamb hung around the kitchen. His mother watched pans on the stove: potatoes and carrots, with steam rising and condensing around plates on the rack above the range. The table was set for three.

Mrs Cooper was searching for something on the bench. "Get the mint for us will y', Gavin?"

Gavin went into the larder and lifted down the jar of dried mint leaves. He unscrewed the cap, sniffed and screwed it back on again. Then he came out and put the mint on the bench.

"Are we gannin' down the garden, after?" Gavin's eyes were turned to his father.

"You're getting just like your father on Saturdays. All you can think about is gardening and going down to that blessed allotment. You don't want to get like yer father." Mrs Cooper began to strain the carrots.

"Well, it's my only chance of getting out of doors, in the whole week," returned Mr Cooper as he bent over the sink and slowly rubbed his hands with soap. "Gavin is good company and he's a good weeder, aren't you, son?" He punctuated the word "aren't" with a prod in Gavin's ribs.

Gavin winced. "Ah like to see the leeks fed."

"We'll be doing that again this afternoon. After dinner," said his father with a friendly grin.

"Aw, smashin'. We're gannin' then."

"Come on, here's y' dinner! Quit gassing, you two!" Mrs Cooper spoke sharply and then brought over the steaming plates. When they were all set on the table, mother, father and son sat down. Mr Cooper began eating, taking good solid mouthfuls. His wife ate fussily, only using a fork. She poked and prodded the lamb. The food seemed to agitate her. Her eyes darted here and there across the table, and she noticed Gavin adding a lot of mint sauce to his meat and potatoes.

"You'll have no insides when you grow up with all those sauces and pickles," she commented.

But Gavin took no notice and only ladled more sauce on his potatoes.

"Stoppit!" She slapped his arm and caused him to splash the cloth with vinegar stains. "Now look what you've done!" She sighed with exasperation, but continued eating.

Mr Cooper seemed to miss the whole episode. He continued eating in his quiet rhythmic way, head down and saying nothing as usual.

Suddenly Gavin jumped up. "Mam, what's for pudding?"

"You've not even finished your meat yet. Anyway Ah didn't have time to make anything today. You'll just have to have an apple or something from the larder." The food on all three plates was disappearing, but on Gavin's plate disappearing rapidly. When it was all over, he got an apple from the box in the larder. They had been given the apples by old Mr Wilkie down at the allotment. He gave them a box every year.

A moment later Gavin was standing in the yard munching the crisp green apple and watching two sparrows fighting on the old wireless aerial, and then his father stepped from the back door.

It was a long walk down to the allotment. They crossed no fields, but they did pass two open spaces where the dirty terraced houses had been pulled down. Next spring, the weeds would invade and colonise, carpeting the rubble, plaster and its dusty soil and hiding the ugly desolation. Then the contractors would arrive, clear and level the site, and erect new flats and houses. For perhaps forty or fifty years the site would be secure, then time would smile again, the houses would be abandoned and the weeds would return to cloak the ground.

Gavin watched an old newspaper fluttering from an upstairs window. "Dad, what are they going to build over there?"

"Ah don't know," said his father, with no interest in his voice, and Gavin pursued the subject no further.

Mr Cooper was not a very tall man and so Gavin was able to walk alongside and keep up with him without much difficulty. As they passed through the gate into the allotment field, a flock of pigeons swung over their heads in tight formation and wheeled away towards a small pigeon loft. A man wearing an old grey cap stood by the loft eyeing his pigeons with an earnest expression on his face. Then after another circular swoop over the footpath, the pigeons, as if ruled by a single mind, alighted on the red spikes on the roof of the pigeon loft. One by one they pushed, cooing, through the wire trapdoor and into the darkness of their cages. The man with the cap picked up a bird gently but firmly, and inspected its opened wings.

"Why do they look at pigeon's wings like that?" asked Gavin.

His father said nothing for a few paces. Then, after a look at the pigeon man, "Ah don't know." Another long pause passed by. "Ah expect they're looking for bugs or something."

"What dee the bugs dee, then?"

"Make it ill, Ah suppose." Mr Cooper became a little agitated. "Ah don't know. Ah've never kept pigeons. You'll have to ask your uncle Arnold. He keeps pigeons."

But again Gavin was satisfied.

In the allotment, Gavin went to look at the jumpy things on the surface of the water in the rain barrel, whilst in the tiny greenhouse his father prepared to feed the leeks.

"Dad, what are these jumpy things?"

"Eh?" His father looked at him through the greenhouse glass. "What, son?"

"These jumpy things in the barrel? What are they? They got little legs and they sort of stick onto the surface. Come and look."

"They're bugs. Ah'll kill them in a minute. Here, you come and get the oil can."

Gavin got the oil can from the shelf underneath the greenhouse table. "Is there any in?" He shook the can against his ear.

"Aye. Well, there's some detergent in the can. One or two drops on the surface. This chokes them and they die."

Outside again, Gavin stood on his toes and pressed a pale green drop of detergent from the can and watched it slowly mingle and disappear in the still water of the barrel. Suddenly and all around, the tiny larvae began to sink into the green and black depths. Some still jumped and twitched as they sank, but soon they had all disappeared from sight. All that remained was the dancing reflection of his father's brown hair and the pale shine of his forehead. Then Mr Cooper crouched down at the cupboard beneath the table.

When he stood up, he began stirring the leek food in an old yellow bulb bowl. His hands were angular and a trifle awkward, a subtle pattern of prominent tendons and swollen veins. As Gavin came into the greenhouse, Mr Cooper hurriedly put a brown packet under the table, but Gavin had spotted him.

"What is your leek food, Dad?"

"Ah'm not telling you or anyone else. It's my secret recipe. Y'd go and tell all the kids at school if Ah told you."

"Ah wouldn't," said Gavin slowly as he ran his fingers through dry sandy soil on the table top. For a few moments, both father and son became absorbed in their separate worlds. One mixing his secret recipe, one doodling on the table top.

Then Mr Cooper broke the spell. "See, son. You gan up to where the onions are and dig it over."

"Up by the seat?"

"Aye. And don't forget to throw the weeds on the heap this time!"

Gavin took the small spade and dug happily for the next half-hour. His father attended to the leeks and fed them with his secret recipe.

All around them in the gardens were tiny greenhouses and huts, one end always covered in old lino or oilcloth. Mr Cooper's was just like the rest, but he was lucky in having a very large rain barrel. In droughts, gardeners from all around borrowed his water for their parched lettuces and tomato plants. This had been a good summer, and even now the sun shone from a blue sky painted with wispy clouds. The leaves in Mr Wilkie's apple tree whispered and rustled in a faint breeze. Near the rain barrel, some chrysanthemums nodded and swung lazily from side to side, as if seeking a better and more open view of the rest of the garden. There was not much left to see, in any case. The potatoes were nearly all finished and only one row lay untouched. Most of the vegetables had been picked or lay wrinkled and dry, and the size of the rubbish heap revealed the most recent activity.

"Next week Ah think we'll burn some of that lot," said Mr Cooper, eyeing the heap of dry and rotting plants.

"Can't we have a fire now?"

"No, we'll have to be going soon. We'll burn it next week."

Minutes later they were passing the pigeon lofts again on their way home.

"Don't you forget to clean your shoes on the bar," said Gavin's father as they closed the door of the backyard.

Gavin scraped his shoes whilst his father put a bag of potatoes in the old coalhouse. Then he ran into the house. "Mam! Mam! We're back!"

His father followed him in. "Mary! We're home!"

"Did you bring back the potatoes?" asked his wife, appearing in the hall doorway.

"Yes, and we'll have some more of old Wilkie's apples by the look of his tree."

"And Ah dug over the patch by the old seat and saw some jumpy things," said Gavin.

Mrs Cooper pressed the kitchen door firmly shut and slowly turned around to face her husband. "Bill," she pronounced his name almost as question, "you know what I was telling you about what Mrs Blenkinsop said the other day?"

"No." Mr Cooper was dragging off his boots.

"You know, about the switches, the plugs."

"Oh, yes." He did not sound very sure.

"How she had hers made into three-pin downstairs and some new ones upstairs."

"Oh aye," sighed Mr Cooper and sank back into the chair. "Ah didn't know she'd had new ones upstairs."

"Well, she did." Mrs Cooper paused again as her husband began to settle deeper into the chair. Soon he would slip off and have a light nap. "Well, Ah thought that we might have a few plugs put in, too."

Mr Cooper yawned. "Yes, alright then. Ah'll see what I can do about it." His eyes closed and his wife waited. Then they flickered open again. "They'll be somebody at work who can do something about it."

Gavin stared at his mother and then down at his father.

His mother looked down at the rug on the floor and then up again at her husband. "Well actually, Ah've already got someone who can do the job."

"Oh well, that's alright then, isn't it...."

"And Ah've asked him to have a look at the old plugs and now he's up on the landing seeing about the new ones upstairs."

Mr Cooper liked his wife to arrange things. "Well, if you got it all organised, then that's all right by me."

Mrs Cooper began to speak just a little faster. "Well, in the circumstances I thought it was best to go ahead and get the man in to look around. He's an electrician who's been staying with a friend of Mrs Blenkinsop's. The Robson's, y' know. He's been trying to get the job on the estate. He's called Mr Wilson."

"How much is it going to cost, then?" asked Mr Cooper, opening the kitchen door and going into the hall.

"Mr Wilson says about twenty pound."

Gavin stayed standing in the kitchen doorway.

"I might be able to do it for eighteen." Mr Wilson leaned over the banister and then came downstairs. He was a youngish man in his twenties, with a healthy brown complexion, a strong even nose and black creamed hair. He wore clean dungarees and a pair of brown pointed shoes. A folding steel-rule stuck out of his dungaree pocket.

"Well, if you can do the job for eighteen pound, that'll be fine. It's really needed doing a while now," said Mr Cooper, looking kindly at his wife.

"That'll be wonderful," agreed Mrs Cooper.

"I always try to do a good job for people," beamed Mr Wilson, displaying even white teeth.

Gavin had been watching Mr Wilson with rather a straight and unimpressed face, but now he smiled.

"When is the best time for you to begin, then?" asked Mr Cooper.

"Well, Ah'll have to work in the evenings."

"Can you start on Monday?" asked Mr Cooper.

"Yes, certainly," beamed Mr Wilson.

Gavin smiled back again. They all moved towards the front door.

"So we'll see you on Monday, then," said Gavin's father, offering his hand.

"Yes, I'll be round about six o'clock." Mr Wilson shook the hand warmly.

"Well, Ah'll be out, but Mary'll fix you up."

"Okay then, and thanks."

The door closed, and Gavin turned and went into the kitchen for tea.

# THREE

Mr Wilson had four plugs to replace downstairs and three new ones to put in upstairs, and so the job took several evenings. He set about his work as soon as he arrived and in a few minutes his tool-bag was open and the neat rows of tools were spread on the canvas. Mrs Cooper noticed that on the first night he spent a long time searching for some screws which had rolled down a crack in the floorboards, so she lent him an old white sheet to work on. This prevented him from losing small pieces of equipment and it also kept the carpets clean.

As he worked he said very little, but sometimes as he clipped wire with his pliers he could be heard whistling quietly. And when he finished at about half past eight, Mrs Cooper always gave him a cup of tea and they talked for a while in the kitchen.

On the first night he came, Gavin was a little wary of him, but his ready smile and friendly manner soon caused Gavin to join him as he worked. At first he simply watched in silence, but soon he was asking questions all about the ins and outs of slipping wires under the floorboards and fitting plugs to the wall. When Mrs Cooper saw this, she told Gavin to mind his own business and leave Mr Wilson alone, but Mr Wilson said he did not mind the lad around because he was always so interested. And so after a day or two, their exact whereabouts in the house was revealed to Gavin's mother by the clink and clatter of tools, the scrambling of wire being pushed through narrow places and the mingling of a young boy's chatter with the electrician's quiet replies.

The tool-bag fascinated Gavin. He loved to slide the spanners and chisels out of their canvas pockets, line them all up in order of size and slide them back in again. "What's this 'un called?"

Mr Wilson stopped turning his brace and bit, and straightened up to stretch his back. "That's an awl."

Gavin looked at it carefully.

"That's used for boring small holes in wood. This big one here is a brace and bit. This is used for drilling large holes.... That one makes a lot of shavings... Yes, that's right, and you're not having them blow all over the landing like you did downstairs."

"Ah won't blow them this time."

"What d' y' want to do with them then?"

"Just collect them."

"What for?"

"Ah don't know. Ah just want to collect them."

"Well, when Ah've finished, you can collect them into a little heap for me and that'll save me the trouble of cleaning them away."

Just then the brace broke through the skirting board and the electrician turned it the other way and withdrew it carefully. He blew away the sawdust to get a better view of his handiwork. Gavin always liked that bit. Then, after being satisfied with the hole, Mr Wilson started to unravel a small coil of thirteen amp wire.

Meanwhile, Gavin wasted no time in collecting the shavings into a heap and crushing them into tiny fragments in his hand. "What are y' going to do with the money which Dad's going to give yer?"

Mr Wilson turned to the small boy and smiled a little. "By, you don't half ask some questions, Gavin lad. Anyhow, Ah've not made my mind up yet." He paused. "Ah think Ah'll buy a stagecoach."

"Oh." Gavin looked very serious. "What are y' going to do with that?"

"Ah don't really know," said Mr Wilson quietly, continuing at his work. "Ah know, Ah shall carry all me jewels in it. Up and down the country."

"Oh. Ah didn't know you were really rich."

"Oh yes, Ah've got thousands, tucked away all over the place."

"Lots and lots?" Gavin's eyes were wide.

"Aye.... No, lad, not really. Ah was only pretending. Don't you ever play let's pretend?"

"That's what girls play," said Gavin very scornfully. "Ah like to play cowas an' indies and gan up into the camp in the fields."

Mr Wilson began to pull the wire down the wall with some string.

"Aren't y' really rich, then?" asked Gavin.

"Well, Ah've got a bit saved up, y' know. When Ah've got a bit more Ah'm hoping to buy a motorbike."

Gavin gasped. "Phew! Dennis's brother's got one. He's in the Air Force. When he comes home, he gives Dennis rides. They gan really fast. About 190 miles an hour. Ah've seen them."

"Not as fast as that."

"Yes, they do, Ah've seen them."

Mr Wilson smiled to himself.

Gavin began destroying his pile of shavings and ran his fingers over the carpet so that they flicked into the air. "If you get one, can Ah have a ride on the back?"

"Not if you don't stop that mess."

The neat pile began to reassemble.

"Well alright, but Ah don't think Ah'll be able to go as fast as Dennis's brother."

"That's all right, as long as you do about 150 or something. Brrrrrrrrrr!" Gavin simulated the noise of a motorbike cornering and changing gear at about 150 miles an hour. With hands gripping invisible handlebars, he revved the engine a few times and then shot off down the street swerving to one side to take another sharp corner.

"Watch what you're doing! You'll knock me over in a minute with your swerving about."

The motorbike disappeared. The hands dropped again. For a few minutes there was silence.

"What're you doing now?"

"You've seen me do this before. Ah'm screwing the wire onto the plug."

"Can I screw the screws in when you've put it on the wall?"

"Yes, if you like. Hell! The bloody screwdriver's slipped again onto my finger. I'll have hands like bloody colanders when I finish this job." He completed the screwing with blood running down his finger and onto his palm. "That's that bit done. Now to screw it here." He sucked his bleeding finger. Afterwards it looked clean and pink compared with the others.

In a few moments the plug socket was safely screwed onto the skirting board. A smear of blood could be seen on one side of the white plastic.

"Come now, Gavin, and get off to bed!"

Neither Mr Wilson nor Gavin had heard Mrs Cooper come up the stairs. They both turned as she noticed the completed plug.

"Oh, you've finished that one! Good."

"Yes," Mr Wilson sucked his finger again. "Yes, we've only the front room now. We should finish that tomorrow."

"Your hand's bleeding."

"No, it's only my finger. The screwdriver keeps slipping."

"Come downstairs and Ah'll put a bandage on for you. Come, Gavin! You go to bed now. And what's that thing you're keeping in the coal-house?"

"Geordie asked me to look after his rabbit. So I'm keeping it in there. Just until the morning."

"You make sure it's gone tomorrow! We don't want rabbits all over the place."

Mr Wilson smiled.

"Anyhow, you get off to bed now! It's late!"

"Ah don't want ter go to bed yet. Cos Ah never go before ten o' clock," said Gavin defiantly.

"You'll do as y're told! I don't want to wallop you in front of Mr

Wilson, but if you don't get a move on Ah shall." Mrs Cooper's voice was hard and angry.

Gavin got up and stooped again to push a spanner back into its canvas pocket. It wasted a little time. His mother looked at Mr Wilson and shook her head slowly.

"Y're always shouting at us," said Gavin as he went into his room, and then more quietly: "Ah hate Mam. Ah'd much rather have Dennis's. I think you're a big hag. Witchy! Witchy!"

"What was that?!" Mrs Cooper ran forward but Gavin slammed the door before she could get near. "Just wait till Ah tell your father about this. Ah'll learn you not to mutter about me."

When she turned around to Mr Wilson, a cynical smile flickered across his lips and he had raised one eyebrow.

"No use telling his father," she continued. "He wouldn't tread on a worm, never mind wallop that...." Words failed her.

Mr Wilson began to laugh a little. "That's what they call having spunk!"

"Ah'd call it rank defiance." She noticed the finger again. "Oh, Ah'd forgotten about your finger. Come down and Ah'll put something on for you." She turned and shouted through the closed door. "And you hurry up and get into the bathroom and off to bed! Don't dawdle in there all night!"

Mr Wilson collected up his tools and followed her down the steep staircase.

Gavin washed himself in a way which he felt was adequate and soon he was sitting up in bed looking at another monster comic. Downstairs, the bandage was being carefully bound and in a dark corner of the coal-house the bundle of white rabbit shivered, her whiskers trembled and her soft pink eyes stared into the darkness, wide and cold. She was hungry and chilled but Gavin had forgotten her, and now he threw the comic aside, ran over to the light, switched it off and bounded into bed. Only a few minutes later, he was sound asleep.

Outside, the darkness was pierced by the singing of people returning from a crowded pub, but their sounds passed through the sleeping boy. Footsteps of returning couples floated through the air, but eventually the streets were silent and the twinkling lamps were alone with the grey and ginger tomcats as they searched around for their mates. And down in the coal-house, the whiskers still trembled and the pink eyes stared into the darkness, stared and grew wider, and wider and deeper, until at last they glared right among the folds of Gavin's dreams.

He opened his eyes and moved under the bedclothes and listened hard. There was no sound at all in the shivering blackness of his room. He closed his eyes again but the pink eyes blinked back, so he pushed back the bedclothes and swung his legs on to the cold floor.

Then he heard a sigh and whimper come through the still house. He sat bolt upright, and his eyes widened and his ears strained. In the coal-house, the rabbit flicked her whiskers at a wandering spider, and little drops of her condensed quick breaths were running down a smooth lump of coal. After a long pause, Gavin heard the sighing again and what sounded like someone's voice. The sound definitely rose from downstairs and already the rabbit was beginning to curl up into a white ball and its eyes were fading as the fear drew across them, until only two grey slits remained.

Very slowly, Gavin slid off the bed, straining his ears in the darkness for any sound, and crept across to his bedroom door. He turned the handle of the door very slowly so that the dry spring sent tiny clinking squeaks into the darkness. Gradually he eased back the door and crept onto the gloomy landing. No street lights shone in from the window and so all was in total darkness.

Taking care to tiptoe past his mother's bedroom, Gavin reached the top of the stairs and just had placed one hand on the banister rail when he heard the noise again, only this time it seemed to finish in a stifled giggle. He hung by the banister, silent and stiffened. The hand on the banister rail became moist. His heart thumped as though it demanded to be heard by the whole house.

Below, the sitting-room door was a little ajar, and he could see a red glow inside. He listened intently again.

"Mary, you've been marvellous to me."

This time he heard the whisper clearly but the reply was inaudible. As he craned over the banister the back of his neck began to prickle.

Suddenly and without any warning he almost ran down the remaining stairs, missing the creaky one near the bottom, and silently tiptoed across the narrow ribbon of red carpet against the door frame. For a second or two he hesitated and then pushed the door open a few inches and slipped his head round.

In the fireplace, the two-bar electric fire was burning, and on the settee in the reddish glow he could see his mother half lying back with Mr Wilson sprawled across her. His face was buried in her neck and his arms were wound tightly around her body. She was smiling as she ran her hands through his hair and over his back. He moaned again, softly. Gavin could see his bare bottom gently moving up and down between her bent legs, and his trousers round his ankles. No one had seen him.

Slung in a crumpled heap in one of the armchairs were his mother's skirt and blouse. The electric fire hummed and hissed as a tiny spark flickered at one end of the filament. The light it made threw a shadow of a moving arm and Mrs Cooper's head on the pale wallpaper pattern.

Gavin saw all this in a few seconds and quickly drew back behind the door again. Without pausing, he ran silently across the hall and up the first few steps. The creak caused by the second step was like a crack of thunder in the quiet house.

"What was that?!"

"What was what? You've bumped my chin sitting up so quickly. Don't be so panicky, Dave. You gave me such a shock. Ah didn't hear anything."

"I'll swear I heard a noise. It sounded like the stairs.... Don't, Mary. Listen!"

Gavin was crouched against the banister, again stiff with fear. His legs in their flexed position began to shake. Again there was a long tense silence.

"Oh, come on, Dave; don't spoil it...."

"Don't, Mary. Listen. What was that?"

In that moment, Gavin ran up the remaining stairs and into his bedroom. He made no sound as he shut the door.

"I'm sure I heard someone running up the stairs. Ah bet it's that kid."

"You're always imagining sounds and things. Gavin is fast asleep in bed. What are you worrying about?" She giggled. "Trouble about you is that you've got a guilty conscience. About us.... You have, you know," she said playfully. "Now, what about me...?"

A long silence followed, in which only the shadows moved on the wallpaper.

"You're a marvellous woman, Mary. I don't know how I've ever done without you. What you make me feel...."

"I love you, Dave. I love you."


"Well, Mr Wilson, y've done a fine job and here's y' money. There's twenty there because Mary's very satisfied with what you've done." Mr Cooper handed over the money and looked very pleased with himself.

"Why, thank you very much, Mr Cooper. I didn't expect this. I only expected eighteen pound."

"Well, that's because Ah got a bit of time off work. Ah'd said I'd be late. Fixed it up with George. Y'see Ah reckoned yer might refuse Mary the extra two pound. Ah wanted to pay yer myself. No refusing. We want you to take it."

Mrs Cooper came in and so all three were now standing in the sitting-room.

"Has he fixed the money with y' alright?" She beckoned the two men to sit down but neither would.

"Yes. I've got much more than I expected. Thank you very much. I don't know how...."

"Aye, well, it was a good job and a good job needs to be paid well," said Mr Cooper, nodding his head.

"Well, thanks very much." Mr Wilson smiled broadly at both of them.

"And what are you going to do with yourself now? Have you got the job on the estate?"

"Yes, I got a job at Aubrey and Fisher the day before yesterday and I start tomorrow. Eleven pound a week."

"So you'll be settling round here for a while, now you're all fixed up?"

"Well, there was one other thing," Mrs Cooper interrupted. "Mrs Robson can't keep him any longer because her son is coming out of the RAF, so I wondered if we could put him up." She did her best to sound quite natural but she was aware of a nervous dryness in her voice.

Mr Cooper stared at her without saying anything.

"We could do with the extra money," she continued, "and we could easily fix up the other front room." She turned to her husband. "What y' think, then?"

Mr Cooper paused for only a moment. "It sounds a fine idea to me. Ah've always thought that front room a bit of a waste. The money can buy you a fridge if you like. Aye, Mr Wilson will be welcome."

Mr Cooper beamed as his wife's face slowly relaxed into a warm smile which she also directed at Mr Wilson.

"Why, thanks very much. It's very good of you. That's really helpful, as it'll save us looking around." Mr Wilson was both pleased and surprised.

Then Gavin came into the room. "Hello, Mr Wilson," he said quietly.

"Hello, Gavin lad," Mr Wilson replied in a very uninterested way.

"What's wrong with you today?" asked Gavin's father.

"Nothing." Gavin was very sullen.

"He's been moody all day. Ah cannot make head nor tail of him," said his mother. "See, Gavin, go and get Mr Wilson's tool-bag."

When Gavin returned with a tool-bag, Mr Wilson was leaving.

Mr Cooper was speaking: "Yes, you can put your motorbike in the backyard if you want. We don't mind. Aye, so we'll see yer in a couple of days time. Ta'ra then!"

"Ta'ra! Ta'ra, Mrs Cooper!"

Gavin went to the door with him, followed him outside and gave him the tool-bag. "When are y' getting yer motorbike?"

"Oh, soon."

"Will y' gisuh ride?"

"Ah don't know. Ah'll have to see." Not waiting for any further comment from Gavin, Mr Wilson turned away and walked briskly down the street, cursing silently.

# FOUR

It was a fortnight later that David Wilson bought his motorbike and brought it back to the Coopers. When he arrived with it, Mr Cooper was out at work and so Gavin and his mother were the first people to see it. It was a fairly new 350cc BSA, and as it stood in the backyard it looked powerful and almost menacing with its paint and chrome gleaming coldly.

Mrs Cooper admired it without understanding all the technical information which Mr Wilson was so eager to tell her.

Gavin stood by his mother, his eyes flashing over the whole machine. He was fascinated. "Can it go as fast as Dennis's brother's?"

"Well, it shows 120 on the speedometer," said Mr Wilson proudly.

Mrs Cooper craned forward to see the instruments more clearly. "But you won't go as fast as that, will you?"

" 'Course he will. He's gan to give us a ride. Ah bet you can gan faster than Dennis's brother. At least 150! Brrrrrrrr!" Gavin again dived into the world of fantasy.

Above Gavin's head, Mrs Cooper and Mr Wilson smiled warmly at each other.

"Well, Ah think it's a lovely machine. And only fifty-five

pounds. It seems very good value to me."

"Yes, it's not bad. Later Ah'll try it out properly, but you can see it start now." Mr Wilson mounted the new motorbike and kicked the engine into a mighty roar. A ginger cat scuttled away from the coal-house roof and over the backyard wall. The motorbike's roar came in bursts now, as Mr Wilson twisted the accelerator. In the dim light, blue smoke drifted around the yard and the smell of exhaust fumes rose in the still air.

As he sat there, he shouted through the noise. "You can tell the engine is in good shape. Listen!" He revved the engine again. "It's just run in right. Only done 6000 miles."

Mrs Cooper nodded and Mr Wilson, taking this as a token of understanding, continued to pour out more enthusiastic technical data. Meanwhile Gavin's face quite simply showed that he was dying to be on the back.

"Do y' want to get on the pillion?" Mr Wilson shouted at Mrs Cooper, as the motorbike engine settled to a steady roar.

"No, Ah can't really."

"Well, you can sit sideways. Come on."

"Oh well, all right." She slipped rather awkwardly onto the seat and put her arms around his waist. He revved the engine in a series of deafening roars. Mrs Cooper laughed a little, partly from exhilaration and partly from fear. She shouted in his ear. "Don't, Dave! That's far too loud."

He turned his head and grinned, revved loudly again and then she touched his shoulder and made a sign that she wished to get off. The engine almost died away and she dismounted.

Gavin wasted no time in asking. "Can I get on the back now?" His wide eyes gleamed with excitement.

Suddenly the motorbike revved loudly again, blue fumes rose into the air and the engine cut. Mr Wilson swung his leg off the bike. The silence rang in everybody's ears.

"Just look at that blue smoke!" Mrs Cooper had only just noticed.

Gavin became rather insistent. "Can't Ah get on the back?"

"Well, it's too late now, I'm putting the bike away. I'll see if I can give you a ride tomorrow." He turned towards Mrs Cooper. "I'll keep it here against the wall. I've got an old cape to put over it."

"It'll be safe enough there."

Mrs Cooper began to move towards the back door, but Gavin wanted to help Mr Wilson put the cape on the bike.

"No, Ah can do it. That's all right."

Gavin let go of the oil-skin and disappointment clouded his face.

"Come on, Gavin! Bed for you! Now!" Mrs Cooper called from the back door.

Gavin ran over to her and looked back at the motorbike. "It's smashin', isn't it? And tomorrow Ah'm having a ride. Mr Wilson says so!"

Next morning it was Saturday and Mr Cooper woke up feeling unwell and so decided to spend his active day in bed. His wife did not mind because this meant he would be out of the way and both she and the allotment would have peace.

Mr Wilson was out at work in the morning, and off so early that Gavin missed the roar of the motorbike as it accelerated in the narrow back lane. As his father remained in bed, Gavin slept in also, and did not get up until almost midday. He had his dinner with his mother. Mr Wilson had not returned and was unlikely to do so before two o'clock.

Mr Cooper had his dinner alone, sitting up in bed. The bedspread was littered with old gardening magazines. When Gavin brought his dad's dinner downstairs, only half eaten, Mrs Cooper knew that her husband really was feeling unwell.

After lunch, Gavin went out to look for Mr Wilson coming home on his motorbike, but the street was empty and so he set off to go and call on Dennis. However, as he got to the end of the street the motorbike screeched around the corner and roared past him. He ran after it. When he arrived, Mr Wilson was bending down and fastening some wires. He did not look up.

"Hello, Mr Wilson," said Gavin rather shyly, but he received no answer. "Is there something wrong with that wire or something?"

Mr Wilson lifted his head and looked at Gavin. His face was not friendly. Then he turned back to finish tightening a terminal. Gavin went round to the other side of the motorbike and put his hands on the handlebars.

"Hey! Who said you could put your hands on the handlebars? It's not your bike, y' know!" Mr Wilson sounded more than a little annoyed.

Gavin let go of the handlebars and looked rather taken aback. He stared for a long time at a cigarette packet in the gutter. "When you've finished can Ah have a ride?"

Mr Wilson continued to bend over his machine.

There was a long silence only broken by the click of a front door and footsteps up the street, as Mrs Bell set off on her weekly expedition to the city shops.

"Can Ah?" asked Gavin in a small voice.

"For hell's sake stop bloody well pestering me! All you've done is follow me around like a sheep, always wanting a ride. Well, you are not bloody well getting one from me!"

At this onslaught from Mr Wilson, Gavin could only back away, staring at him. "But yer promised us!"

"Ah promised yer nothing! Gan away will y', before Ah have to dee something to you! Gan on, buzz off!" shouted Mr Wilson, his face pale.

Gavin turned and, almost crying, ran down the street. He did not look around but ran on round the corner of the houses, and then the soft salt tears ran across his cheeks and made streaks in the dirt on his face. He was running towards Dennis's but after a while he settled down to a walk. When he came to the end of Craster Avenue he turned away for some reason, and began running again. He did not stop until he had made his way up to the old railway siding on the embankment. Here there was no one else around, and so when he sat down he was alone with the humming of a bee moving from one plant to another. Flowers and green stuff seemed to thrive in between the old tar-covered sleepers.

He was sitting beside the railway track. Some shunting must have taken place recently because the steel rail was shining and grey with only a streak of rust here and there. The sun was high and the rail was warm.

Nearly half a mile away in the distance was the Jubilee Pit. It was an old colliery now, threatened with closure. Dirty redbrick buildings were clustered round grim girders of the pithead. Beyond the ventilation building, a tall chimney poured out treacly black smoke. Beneath, there was a network of shining rails littered with coal trucks. But the stark shapes of the pithead buildings were softened a little by a belt of woodland on the hillside behind.

Between Gavin and the pit was an area of barren uneven slag heap. No plants grew in the hostile shale and only in the spring was some of the area covered in dry spiky grass. Over to the right, the newest part of the slag heap rose as a conical hill of debris. Tiny trucks rolled up a funicular railway and tipped more slag over the top. The stones and shale went rattling and rolling down the steep sides until they came to rest.

Here and there, disused railway trucks and sidings crept in and out of the hillocks of slag. In some places, the soft grey rock had slipped from underneath the railway, and the lines and sleepers had buckled and twisted themselves into grotesque shapes and design. The whole area of slag was unfriendly, sterile, and barren. In hot weather it was almost impossible to walk over the hot rock and most of the kids kept well away from the heap.

As Gavin surveyed the scene in front of him, he suddenly became aware of a column of black smoke rising from behind a low hill of shaley soil. The smoke did not drift as there was little wind, but instead it rose as a writhing black pillar gradually intermingling with the blue sky until, bluer and bluer, it could no longer be seen.

Gavin got up and raced down the embankment, crashing through the bushes of rusty sorrel. At the top of the next hillock he could see a large grass fire with flames licking across the ground, engulfing the dry yellow grass. He scrambled down the slippery rocks of the hill and across to the front of the fire, which stretched for about thirty feet.

The burning sorrel and grass hissed and crackled. Twisted dried stems spat and sang, untwisted hideously and cracked open only to burn along with rest. The area of grass which was already burned smouldered, blue smoke rose, and tiny pieces of burnt grass, now infinitely light, settled and flickered with a thousand spots of red light.

As the fire burned its way across the grass, Gavin could see a man and a dog standing a few yards away, previously quite hidden by the smoke. He moved across to the man, who was wearing a rather old-fashioned dark suit over a dirty white open-necked shirt. The suit flapped loosely around him and his shirt had no collar.

His dog was a beautiful big collie which noticed Gavin coming towards them. He flicked his tail and his master looked up.

"Hello, son. Ah didn't see y' coming." The man had a kindly smile. "It's a canny big open fire, isn't it?"

Gavin did not reply. The fire was reaching the end of the grass now and the crackling and spitting was beginning to die down.

"It's dying away now. Soon it'll be finished.... Here boy! Stay!" The keen eyes of his dog had spotted something on the hill and in response had started forward, but his master called him back. The dog returned immediately to his former position and then flicked a glance at its master, who nodded and smiled back. There was silver stubble covering the man's chin and his cheeks were patterned with tiny interlacing blood vessels. He had obviously spent a great deal of time in the open air. When he spoke, his voice had a full rich and yet quiet sound, a sound which was close to the hills of the north of the county. It was friendly and invited conversation.

"Ah saw the fire and came running over."

"Aye, Ah hesn't seen a one like this before. Not here, like. Seen bigger 'uns up at Cremlington though." The man's blue eyes twinkled and the guttural r's rolled in the back of his throat.

Gavin looked away from the fire and up at the man. The sun was just on the man's shoulder and it made Gavin squint and put his head on one side. "What caused the fire, Mista?"

"An owd bornin' hoal, ower there." He pointed to a hole in the ground about sixty feet away.

They walked over to it. It was almost four feet across and around it was soft dusty-red cinder ash. Inside, it twisted down red and hot, its walls covered in glowing coals. The hot air which rushed out caught their breaths and dried their throats. Gavin looked at the burning hole, fascinated, whilst the man held back the dog and put him on the lead.

"Where does it gan tee, Mista?"

The old man's eyes twinkled again, and he screwed them up a few times against the blinding heat. "They gan deep into the ground. Thear, thear's a greeat underground fire. This sort of lets the smoke and gas escape."

"Does it gan down far?"

"Nurbody really knurs. It just twists doon into th'earth. They say it's the hot coal that got chucked out of the pit that does it. It's aalways warm roond here. Y' see ower there, there's some smaller hoals. Sometimes they gan out but later others start off. The coals gan on borning in the hoal until the walls tumble in. Y' knar, it aal crumbles." He made a sign with his hands which described the action.

Gavin stroked the head of the collie, who nuzzled up to him and began to lick his hand.

"When the fire and fumes jumps out of the hoal it lights the grass and stuff. That's what happened here. This is one of the biggest that Ah've ever seen here, though."

"Hev y' seen other ones then?"

"Oh aye. They're quite common up at Cremlington where Ah used to be a pitman. There was some really big ones. Y' knar, aboot five to six feet across. An' bornin' coals aall ower the place and sulphur and hot gases. Y' could light a tab easily. In winter after the snow had fallen y' could aalways tell the bornin' heaps. That's what we called them. Because the snow melted off them long before anywhere else." The old pitman turned away from looking down the hole and watched Gavin stroking the collie.

"That's Billie. He used to be a sheepdog up at Alnwick but he's retired now so I keep him. He lives with me, don't you boy?" He gave his dog a friendly rub and pat.

"He's a smashin' dog. Like Lassie on the telly."

"Aye, Ah knar, and he's aall Ah've got now. My good lady passed on two winters ago. Now there's just me and Billie." For a few moments the old man became thoughtful and looked towards the pit in the distance. "She'd be alive now if it weren't for yous."

"What did yer say, Mista?"

"Ah was just saying me wife would be alive now if it hadn't been for the owd Jubilee Pit. Ah came here for work. Redundant within a year. The wife went oot to work to make ends meet. Aall that scratting and slaving killed her."

"Did she die quickly then?"

"Aye, it was her heart, y' see."

"My grandad's got a heart."

"It's a terrible business, son. Believe me, it's a terrible business." His voice became very quiet and almost a whisper at the end of this last sentence. Then suddenly he seemed to wake up, looked towards the row of pit cottages on the hill and smiled down at Gavin. "Well son, Ah must be ganning now. Billie and me have a long walk home for tea. Ah expect yours will be ready too. But mebbees we'll see yer again."

He took his dog and shuffled off into the smoke, but when he saw that Gavin had not moved at all, he turned and smiled again. "Ta'ra, son."

"Ta'ra, Mista," replied Gavin slowly, taking another long look down the hole and listening to the hot air roaring as it rushed out into the open.

All around him dead burnt grass smouldered silently. Between the dancing wreaths of smoke, the hot coals glowed amongst the flicks and spurts of flame. Like yellow-red jewels, forbidden, they hung there waiting to be picked off, clustering together in the deeper parts of the tube until, far below, their separate glimmerings were lost in the solid red heat. As Gavin craned over to get a better view, part of the cindery rim of the hole collapsed and fell into the fiery depths. A cloud of sparks was flung into the air and then Gavin was running back over the shaley hillocks, bounding through the sorrel, on his way home for his tea.

As Gavin reached the end of the back lane, he heard a motorbike rev up and roar off in the front street. It sounded like Mr Wilson, so Gavin ran as fast as he could into the backyard. Immediately he was greeted by shouting from inside.

"Ah bet you've been playing around with the bugger, all the time he's been here!"

It was his father. Gavin rarely heard him shout like that.

His mother's voice was strained. She was almost screaming. "There's been nothing between us."

"Divvn't talk daft, woman! Ah saw you and him on that sofa only minutes ago!"

"Don't you believe me? Y've got it all wrong!" His mother appealed. "Ah never did!"

"Don't never me! Mary, I never thought Ah'd call you this but you're a slut, woman, a slut! And you know what they deserve!" With a curious coolness he struck her across the face.

His wife screamed. "Don't you dare hit me, Billy Cooper! Don't you dare hit your wife again."

But it made no difference. There was a wild and distant look in Mr Cooper's eyes as he struck her down to the ground. So measured was his passion, so economic were his blows, that each one counted. But he merely struck her to the ground. There were none in excess.

She lay before him moaning and sobbing, but already the effort of control had made him red in the face and he was becoming short of breath. Gavin, who had been hanging back in the open door, now entered the room, but a glance from his father caused him to cower by the wall.

"What d'you want, y' little bugger?! Where've yer been?!"

Gavin's shivering broke into deep gulped sobs.

"If you want your mother you can have her! She's a dirty slut! Tell anybody! Anybody!" He was at the end of his breath and almost wheezing.

Mrs Cooper rolled over and began to get up. Her eyes were wet and a red mark could be seen spreading across her left cheek. She had become hysterical and yet her words came slowly. "No, Billy. No, Billy.... D'y' know why Ah had him? D'y' know why Ah gan to bed with him? Do yer? Do yer?!"

This new outburst took Mr Cooper rather by surprise. He took a step back and raised his hand. For a moment it hung there, and then with a conscious effort he controlled himself. "Stop shouting, woman! Stop shouting! Pull yerself together! Don't shout at me like that!"

In his eyes there was a flicker of uneasiness, but she continued shouting. "It was because ye were no good! Ye don't know how to satisfy a woman! Ye don't know what love really is! Ye couldn't know how to satisfy anything! Anything!" At this point her words became lost in a flood of indistinguishable and hysterical sound. She fell to the floor and began beating the carpet with her hand.

"Shut up, woman! For god's sake shut up!"

Gavin was too frightened to cry properly. His body shook as his whining turned into a long wail.

"Oh, bloody hell! Shut up! Don't you start too!" shouted his father. Mr Cooper caught his breath and looked uneasy. He bent over his wife and tried to pull her hands from her face. "Stop screaming, woman! Please stop screaming like that! Please Mary, Ah can't stand it much longer!"

As he bent over her, Gavin ran past him and upstairs. Long after his bedroom door had slammed, his sobbing could be heard downstairs and it was nearly ten minutes later when he opened the bedroom door and crept onto the landing. He was still sobbing a little. Downstairs his parents were still shouting at each other, but thankfully his mother had stopped screaming.

"Ah come downstairs for an aspirin and what do I find?  You

mucking about on the sofa with that-"

"Ah wasn't doing what y'-"

"Well, what the hell were you doing?"

Gavin saw the door of Mr Wilson's room was open. He walked in and looked around. Mr Wilson had left in a hurry. The bed was unmade. An ornamental jug was smashed on the floor. Over on the table lay an ashtray containing cigarette ends and a cufflink with a gold lion crest. Another cufflink and a few cigarette ends were scattered on the tabletop. Leaning against a pot rabbit on the mantelpiece was a piece of paper with writing on.

Gavin picked up the paper. He could make out the writing of the signature. He took it downstairs to his parents.

They were quieter now, and Mrs Cooper was sitting in the chair by the fireplace. As with all written messages and letters, he took it to his mother.

"This was upstairs, Mam," he said in a small voice.

"Give it to me! Quickly!" She snatched it from his hand, read it and then burst into a series of sobbing cries.

"Shut up, woman! For hell's sake, shut up blubbering! Don't start all that again!"

Gavin bent over to his mother. "Will he be coming back, mam? Mr Wilson, Ah mean?"

She shook her head between sobs.

Gavin burst into tears and ran from the room. "Never come back. And he promised to gisuh ride! And he never gisuh one! He never gisuh one!" He began beating on the stair carpet in a fury.

Mr Cooper was exhausted with arguing and stood leaning against the mantelpiece. The renewed sobbing and wailing sounded throughout the house and at last his patience ran out. "Oh bloody hell! What a home!" He made for the door, slammed it shut, slammed the back door and made off to pay one of his rare visits to the pub.

# FIVE

"Mam?" Gavin walked slowly round the table and slid his hand along the edge and around the corner. There was no reply from his mother. She was ironing with her back to him. "Mam?"

"What?" She sounded on edge and tired. The ironing board creaked as the heavy iron slipped along the warm smooth cloth.

"Can Ah have some money ter gan ter the pictures?"

Mrs Cooper seemed not to have heard.

"Can Ah?" he repeated, more softly and unsure.

"What do y' want to go and see this time?"

"It's with Dennis and the gang. It's on at the Plaza. 'Marcus and the Gladiators'."

His mother looked at him for the first time. Brown hair was showing plainly through her blonde rinse. "Ah thought you'd stopped going round with Dennis."

"That was yesterday."

"That's what you always say. One moment you're all friends, next minute you come in crying. You never used a quarrel like that. Ah don't know what you kids get up to."

Gavin said nothing and began to stare at his mother's carpet slippers by the chair.

She started to iron another of his father's white shirts. "Ah think you ought to decide to be friends with them or not to be friends. Ah'm not going to fight your battles for you. It's your life and you must learn yourself. But Ah wish you'd stop coming in crying your eyes out. Always quarrelling. Ah don't know."

"Sometimes they're all right."

She carefully ironed the cloth between the buttons. "Well, then what happens?"

"They gerrat me."

"Well, what do they gerrat you about?"

Gavin looked away.

"Well of course if yer won't tell me what they do to you, Ah can't help you. Do they gerrat anyone else? You should belt them back if they hit you."

"No, just me." There was a pause. "Mam, can Ah gan ter the pictures?"

"Last time I gave you money for the pictures, y' came in saying they'd pinched it off you. I'm not having that every time you go out. Was it the same lads who get at you?"

"Aye."

"What about, then? Have yer been cheeky to them? Cos you know what to expect, don't you?"

"Na, Ah've not been cheeky."

"Well, you're not getting any money for the pictures until you tell me what it is."

Again Gavin turned away from his mother. There was a short silence and then he remembered. "Can Ah...?"

"Well?"

His mother was becoming impatient. Soon she would lose her temper. Gavin saw the look in her eyes. He spoke slowly and sullenly. "About Mr Wilson." His eyes were fixated on the floor.

"Oh, that's it. Ah could've guessed as much. What have you been saying to them? You should keep your trap shut."

"Ah never said nothing to them."

She grabbed hold of his coat and pulled it tight around his body and shook him. "Well, what did you tell them, eh?"

"Nowt! Nowt!"

"Don't try and nowt me," his mother hissed.

"Nowt. Honest. Nowt!" cried Gavin. "Just that Mr Wilson was ill that night and how he groaned. Ah was just going to feed Geordie's rabbit and-"

"And what?"

"Then the lads began laffin' at us."

Mrs Cooper thrust him away at arm's length, and then she lunged out and struck him hard across the face and arm. "Damn you! You did see us that night! Y' little sneaking bugger! That's why he left! Now Ah know! You ruined everything! Gerrout, damn you. Get out!" she screamed at him as he fled for the door.

"Can Ah gan ter the pictures then?"

"No, you can not!"

He began to wail.

"You dirty snooper! Get out! You're a filthy little bugger, you are!" And as his mother began shouting and screaming again, Gavin ran down the street, his face and arm throbbing with the pain.

"Are ye gannin' then?" It was Jimmy Silver, one of the bigger lads.

"Na. Me Mam winna gis the money." Gavin was breathless with running. His face was tear-streaked.

"Ye've been crying. What have yer been blubbering about this time, eh?"

"Nothing. Ah haven't been crying," said Gavin, rubbing his moist cheeks with the back of his hand.

"Stupid little bugger, that Gavin Cooper." The bigger lads began to laugh amongst themselves.

Dennis and Billy Walker came walking up. "Are y' gannin' then?"

"Na. Me Mam winna gis the money."

"Oh. She never gives ye money now, does she? You should do a paper round like Ah dee." Billy was very proud of his earned money.

"You divvn't dee a paper round! You only help George Parker dee his. And he gives you three shillin' of his money."

"Aye. But one day Ah'll dee his round," said Billy firmly.

"Ye'll never dee George Parker's round," shouted one of the big lads, "because he'll never get a job. Spends too much time smoking fags. He'll gan with the cancer, like. That's what me mam says."

"Ah'm nivvor gan to smoke tabs," remarked Gavin.

"Ye just wait till y're older, lad," said another big lad in a mocking fashion, "then ye'll not be able to keep away from them." And he burst into a fit of horrible laughter.

"Well, we'd better be gannin' then, if we're gannin'." Dennis, with money, was getting impatient. "Come on, Billy!" The two of them started down the street towards the Plaza.

The neon lights of the cinema could be seen a quarter of a mile away down the long straight grey road. The sky was open and cleansed with the cold violet blue that comes with the dark. Already some stars were out and soon the pale light of the mercury lamps would bathe the streets in an artificial moonlight. A breeze blew chillness around the group of boys and promised a heavy dew. Dennis and Billy began to walk faster.

Gavin was left with the four big lads. They were about eleven, and Ben Watson, the one with a ready and foul laughter, was nearly thirteen. He had been at William Squire School for over a year now. That's where all the big lads went.

"Are ye gannin' down to the pictures, then?" asked a ginger-haired lad called Leslie.

"Nah," said Ben. "Ah've seen it already."

"What yer gan ter dee, then?"

"Ah divvn't knar." He paused. "Unless we gan up to the woods and see if they's any lads with their lasses."

"Aye, lads, let's gan up. We haven't been up there for a while now!"

The four boys moved off up the road, away from the Plaza, and soon they began to walk more quickly. For a few moments, Gavin, who had been ignored by them, was left alone. Suddenly he ran and caught up with them.

Leslie looked round at him. "What d' ye want?"

"Can Ah come with y's?"

"Na. We divvn't want little lads with us, do we, Ben?" Leslie cocked an eye and Ben grinned.

"Na, we divvn't, but he can come along if he wants. He couldn't harm anyone. Just remember one thing. You divvn't make a sound, see?"

A quarter of an hour later the group of lads was walking down the cinder-path towards the woods. The sky was clear, the stars were sharp and piercing, and a pale silver crescent was just becoming visible on the horizon behind them. A soft shimmering light filtered through the smog of the town. The chill air was like knives digging in their flesh and the group hurried on to keep warm, around them a cloud of condensed breath. The mercury lamps on the road were far away now. Only the rising moon lit their path, throwing long shadows on the sparkling cinders and revealing in a cold grey light the dark secrets of the hawthorn hedge.

For two hundred yards the path was straight and level. Then there was a broken stile covered with amorous half-literate carvings and crude obscene art, the two often curiously mixed up with each other. Two of the lads stepped over the stile. Gavin and the other two lifted the thick galvanised fence wire, dripping with dew, and crawled through by the side of the stile.

Soon the path steepened, and dark leafless trees began to fill the space in front of them. Then the trees were at their sides, and then all around them. Soon the boys were deep in the wood. Here the moon did not penetrate; dampness and mist hung around the black wet boughs. In the steeper places, twisted roots formed natural steps. The silence in the wood was even more pronounced than in the fields. The dead leaves were too damp and dew-laden to even crackle under their feet.

They all stopped on a little leaf-covered ridge. Very faintly, they could hear the burn far below them, trickling deep beneath the dead bracken fronds. In a huddle of vaporous haloes, they began to talk quietly.

"Where d' y' think they might be tonight?"

"Divvn't knar."

"Bit farther down. By the old log."

"Perhaps. It's a bit cold tonight."

"Don't be daft, man. Cold doesn't make any difference to some of these lads when they get a lass!" laughed Leslie.

"Alright. Gan down a bit further."

They slithered a bit further down the steep bank until without warning, Leslie turned round. "Howay, lads!" he whispered. "Stop! Stop, man! Ah can see someone! Look there!" He pointed between the gloomy trees down to the lower path.

"Aye, Ah can see them," whispered Ben.

They all craned forwards on their knees and stared into the darkness. The couple on the lower path were walking slowly along, linked closely together, arm in arm. The young man was looking down into the face of the girl and speaking softly. She was smiling at his speeches and gazing intently into his eyes. Sometimes her face would turn away and she would giggle a little reply. They walked very, very slowly.

When they got to a spot on the path almost beneath the boys, they slipped feeling arms around each other and kissed for a long time.

Twenty feet above, Leslie and Ben held their breath, whilst the younger ones were sure that the beating of their hearts and their fast breathing would reveal their hiding place. For several minutes they watched in silence as lipstick and powder gradually transferred from one skin to another. Sighs and whispers rose in the still damp air and hands wandered over dark nylon raincoat, over smooth warm skin, until softly she whispered against his cheek, "No, Roddy. No, no more... No, it's too cold."

"What's the matter? You were alright the other night."

"Ah know, but it was warmer then. And you know Ah hev to be home by nine." She left his cheek and looked straight up at his face.

"Aw, alright...." His words trailed off as they had a last kiss. Then gradually they slipped apart and, turning, walked slowly down the leaf-strewn path.

Ben whispered excitedly. "Just a little bit longer and they'd have been really warmed up. He was just gan ter feel her."

"Aye, Ah knar, but we wouldn't have seen anything. You never dee on nights like this."

Gavin looked up at Leslie's shadowy face. "Have yer been to the woods often, like?"

"Why yes. We used to come down here just about every neet, didn't we? Eh, Ben? Last summer."

"Aye. We saw all sorts down here then."

"Much better than tonight. We seen loads of people, sometimes really near. Sometimes about two feet."

They all clambered down onto the path, and their whispers were replaced by ordinary speech.

"Aye. We seen Harry Andrew's sister. Y' knar Harry Andrews?"

Gavin nodded eagerly.

"Why, we've seen his sister Julia down here with her lad. And Elsie Springwell with Tony Marsden."

"Aye. Elsie Springwell.... They were good. She opened her blouse. We seen her titties."

"Aye. And y' knar when yer Mam was gannin' with that electrician with the motorbike. We seen her down with him once."

"Over by that fallen log there," said another lad, pointing to a huge log which straddled the glade.

Gavin looked at the log, and Leslie watched his face closely.

"Me Mam never come down here!" Gavin called out sharply. His little cry seemed to penetrate the trees and fill the whole wood.

"But we seen her," said Leslie smoothly.

"You couldn't! She never come!"

"She was on that log with that electrician. Sitting there. Ah saw her, man. Don't argue." Ben was indignant. Ben could never be quite so controlled as Leslie. He had seen and that was enough.

"She never come here! She-"

"Now look, kidder." Ben grabbed Gavin by the arm. "Divvn't be mistaken! She was bloody well there! You understand?"

Leslie began to smile. "Aw! Let him down!"

Ben released his grip on Gavin's arm, and it was not until they were all quiet and walking down the path that Gavin spoke again. "He had a smashin' motorbike. He gave us loads of rides."

"Ah thought you said the other day he nivvor lived with yer," gibed Ben, grinning at Leslie.

"Well, he only lived with us a short time-"

"Before his father found out!" cut in Leslie.

"Anyhow," continued Ben, "one of the Cochrane lads saw her the other day in The Fusilier with a lad from the works."

"He didn't, cos she never gans near The Fusilier," said Gavin forcefully.

"Whey, but he saw her, man!" shouted Leslie, with the others nodding.

"She never gans there though! She's always in the house, and me and me Dad gans to the allotment and...." He stopped.

They all became silent again. The burn was trickling and gurgling around mossy stones and into hidden dark places. They were all listening to its lonely sounds when Gavin began a new conversation. "Are y' gannin' to the match on Sat'day?"

"Divvn't knar. Might." Ben's voice was devoid of any interest.

Soon they had come to the end of the path, leaving the wood behind them. Their conversation had joined the countless other intrigues that hung in the gloomy mist and on the wet boughs.

"Come on, hurry up, lad! Get a move on! It'll be cold. Ah didn't just cook it to go cold, you know."

Gavin was eating his Saturday dinner. It was nearly two o' clock and he was late because he had spent all morning in the fields making a camp with the gang. One by one they had left him as he dug away sods of earth to make the walls, off to their dinners. It was only when he'd been working alone for nearly half an hour that he realised that he was the only one left. He had run down to the road and through the estate, but it made no difference. He was late.

Slowly he stirred raspberry jam into the cold semolina and began eating it, running his spoon through it to make little furrows.

"Come on! Don't play with yer food, eat it or get outside! Come on! Ah want to gan out this afternoon."

As usual these days, Mrs Cooper had either lost her temper or was about to. Gavin pushed the half-eaten semolina away from him over the plastic table fabric.

"Well? What's wrong with it?"

"Nothing," said Gavin in a tired whisper.

"Well, why don't you eat it then?! Eh? If there's nothing wrong with it."

"It's cold," whispered Gavin.

"That's right! It's cold!" She grabbed him and pulled him out of the chair. "And do you know why it's cold now? Cos you were late!"

Gavin put his arm up to shield him from the expected blows, but they did not come. His mother only shook him by the shirt and jacket.

"Ah don't know why I bother cooking for you lot. One takes his meal and goes off to his bloody allotment without even a word of thanks, and the other comes in late! You make sure it doesn't happen again, d' y' hear me!"

But Gavin had struggled free. He ran out through the back door.

For a moment, his mother stood staring at the door, breathing heavily, then she saw the time on the clock ticking on the mantelpiece. "You'll just have to wash the dishes yourselves. Ah'm going out for a bit of my own pleasure." She spoke loudly to herself, glanced at the clock again and went upstairs to get ready.

When Gavin saw his father, he was halfway to the allotment, striding along Duchess Road. In order to reach him, Gavin took a shortcut and ran across the derelict ground where they'd been pulling houses down. He was running so fast that when he got to his father he ran some steps ahead, and his plimsolls slapped on the hard concrete.

"Hello, son. Where've you been?"

"Just had me dinner."

Mr Cooper smiled to himself. "Ah bet your Mam wasn't very pleased about that!"

"Dad, what are we going to do today?"

"Ah don't know. First we'll have a look around and see."

Gavin looked up at his father and smiled. His father did not smile back but his face looked kind. For a minute or two they walked in silence and Gavin tried to miss all the cracks in the pavement and only walk on the slabs.

His father noticed the boy's concentration on the passing stones. "Yer divvn't want to do that all day long. Y'll trip and break your back."

"Ah've not broken me back yet."

"Aye. But y' will one day if you go on like that."

Gavin lifted his head up slowly and looked straight ahead of him, and they came to the long path down amongst the allotments. As they walked along, Gavin slipped his hand into his father's, and his father's hand clenched. Gavin felt a rough warm glow spread into his own hand. Ahead of them the pigeons drew their tight circles in the sky.

Mr Cooper began speaking. "Anyhow, Ah thought you were ganning to the match this afternoon.... You're holding my hand!" His voice had become quite incredulous. "When did you take hold of it? Ah cannot remember taking hold of yours."

"Ah don't know."

Suddenly they both felt awkward. Gavin looked away.

"We can't have this. It's little lassies what hold their daddy's hand. Ah haven't held your hand since you was a bairn, just walking. You're a big lad now."

Their hands fell apart and they continued walking down the path, whilst beside his hut the pigeon man shook his tin of beans, and overhead the pigeons wheeled round and round.

# SIX

Time slipped past and the year wore on. Evenings grew shorter again and frosts hardened the ground. Mr Cooper had little or nothing to do in the allotment. This did not stop him from going down every Saturday afternoon regular as ever, but when he got there he did not dig or tidy up. Instead, he would sit on his wooden seat smoking cigarette after cigarette, and waiting for the late afternoon and his tea. And as the mists of evening rolled over the lower gardens and made haloes around the rows of old gas lamps along the allotment cinder-path, he would get up, close the greenhouse and set off for home. Usually Gavin was with him, and when they arrived back in Bolton Street they would announce their homecoming in the same old manner, but they would not always receive an answer.

Nowadays Mrs Cooper often spent a few days away from home. She did not give any warning, she would just disappear and reappear two or three days later. Mr Cooper made no bones about his wife's comings and goings. In fact, his lined face, nostrils lazily trickling cigarette smoke, gave no indication whatsoever that he even noticed. Mrs Cooper always told everybody that she had an ill brother on the other side of town. And her friends had become fewer. The neighbours never knew when she would be in.

And they had heard other versions of the story and many were prepared to believe them. But this made little difference to Mr Cooper. He had no interest in the neighbours and hardly knew their names. When his wife was away, he simply had more time to be on his own and in the allotment.

While his mother was away in the day and his father was asleep, Gavin was free to do as he pleased. He took his freedom and played into the mornings before school, often playing in the fields, and sometimes time deserted him and he played into school hours. None of his teachers seemed to notice, nobody was in at home, and soon Gavin was spending whole days away from school, and his time was his own.

During the wet days of November it was different. Mrs Cooper was away as usual, but Gavin did not always spend all day in the fields. It was often too wet and cold. So he went to school where there was warmth and a good hot dinner. The staff noticed that his days "off with colds" were less frequent and they took this as a sign that Gavin had mended his ways. Term broke up in crisp December weather and then there were only a few days to Christmas.

The festive season came and went, pushing before it New Year and leaving in its wake empty beer bottles, headaches, empty aspirin bottles, sore knuckles, torn paper-chains and a recurrent and universally crippling indigestion. Christmas passed by the Coopers and caused gifts to be exchanged, scant smiles to be given, but these all disappeared on Boxing Day when Mrs Cooper learned that her husband had to work in the early afternoon. Already the trigger of Gavin's new ray gun was slipping and in a few days it would jam irreparably.

On the fourth day of Christmas, all fireside family closeness had completely gone and life was almost back to normal. Normality in fact returned on the sixth day when Mrs Cooper took one of her holidays, not returning until late on New Year's Day.

The last trace of Christmas left the neighbourhood when the little green van arrived at the end of the street and the man with the mops and paste began sticking a rural margarine advert on top of a whisky bottle surrounded by tinsel and glass balls. The shadowy figures of an elegant party beyond were replaced by a herd of Jersey cows browsing in a Wiltshire field. When the last half-cow and thatched cottage had found its other half, the little man gave the bill a last rub with his mop and then climbed down the ladder and lifted it onto the roof-rack of his van. Soon the van started up and disappeared down the street, with the paste still damp and tacky.

Every month the van came and the bills were changed or renewed. Margarine was replaced by cigarettes, cigarettes were replaced by furniture polish, and furniture polish was replaced by chocolates. Poking out of the black and white chocolate box were two chicks and all around there were coloured chocolate eggs in silver paper.

As the little man plied his mop and the last glimpses of polished tabletop disappeared forever, Gavin slipped his finger into the paste bucket and drew it out. Little translucent beads dribbled and ran from his finger onto the ground. He had been watching for quite some time with his head on his side, staring upwards, one eye half-closed against the sun. In his hand he held the string of his bogey cart. This was a collection of old pram wheels, wood from orange boxes, and a huge ugly bolt that he had got from a lad whose father worked down in the shipyard.

The little man with the mop looked down at him. "Hey, son! What do you want?!"

"Ah'm just watching yer, Mista."

"Aye, well, just keep away from that bucket!" He waved the mop over Gavin's head and a million tiny droplets sped through the air, catching the light and becoming for a fleeting second particles of scintillation and beauty, before being dashed to the pavement as a meaningless pattern of dirty stains.

The man winked at Gavin, descended the ladder, loudly snooked away catarrhal excess and wiped his nose against the green overall of his sleeve. He was wearing old National Health glasses and his hatchet-shaped face had become wizened and brown with sun and soot. As he lifted his ladder onto the roof-rack of the van, Gavin began to pull his bogey up the street.

"Hey, son! Shouldn't you be at school?"

Gavin hurried on.

"Eeh, Ah divvn't knar what the kids of today will get up to next." He slammed the van door.

When the van passed Gavin, he was already halfway up the long climb to the top of the street. At the top it was different, and the old dirty brick houses stopped and the gable end of each street was now covered in sienna-coloured cement. One of the ends had huge diagonal beams braced up against the cement-covered wall.

In front of Gavin and spread across the flat valley were the factories of the trading estate. Dozens of long low one- and two-storeyed factory buildings were interspaced with straight white concrete roads and larger areas of close-cropped grass, sports fields and car parks. The mid-afternoon sun caught the colours and chrome of parked Fords and delivery-vans sprinkled over the car parks and loading bays. A few factories had railway sidings and were surrounded by neat planned gardens. There was no noise, no blast furnaces or heavy machinery. Plastics, transistors and knitting-wools needed none of that vulgar raw display of industry, and so, rather than being a scene of cramped buildings, smoke and chimney-stacks externally racked by the roar of machinery, the trading estate spread itself over the broad valley in tidy rows, and the hungry production lines and conveyor belts quietly rattled and purred.

Away over to the right lay the city, sprawled over the banks of the river, churches and warehouses poking through the amorphous mass of houses, stretching into the light blue haze on the horizon. The silver of the river wound into the thick smoke haze, and the cooling towers and power station buildings could be seen standing sentinel to the countryside far beyond. A tug screamed on the river below, as a hopper, low in the water, nosed away from the coal staithes and moved downriver towards the city bridges. Beyond, dockside cranes, warehouses and the fine grey line of the sea.

Leading down to the estate was a new concrete road. Builders' materials, water pipes and a contractor's sign were lying on the grass opposite where Gavin was standing. Houses would soon follow.

For a few moments, Gavin sat on his bogey contemplating the panorama in front of him, and then with a grunt he gave himself a push off and was soon speeding down the hill. Near the bottom he ran off the road onto some smooth grass and with his pram wheels rattling on the turf he made a high-speed turn and lurched to a halt.

Now he had to pull the bogey back up the hill. He looked up at the rows of houses above him and spied a tiny figure at the top. He shouted and waved his arm. "Alfie!"

The figure shouted back and began to speed down the hill on another bogey. Gavin watched the moving speck grow in size until with a rattle the bogey was alongside him and going a lot faster than he had. Alfie tried to make a sharp turn but his bogey was too high off the ground, and in a flash he was on his back, legs flying. Over in some thick grass, the wheels of the bogey continued to spin and rattle.

"Yer were gannin' too fast," cried Gavin.

"Ah wasn't, man. Ah just tried to turn too sharp," replied Alfie, re-righting his bogey and then sitting on it.

"Have y' been here long?"

"Na. Just come."

"Have ye been off school all day then?"

"Aye. Me Mam's away."

"See, Ah said ye'd be able to gerroff," said Alfie grinning.

"Aye. Ah've been off before, y' knar."

Alfie pulled out a packet of chewing gum, put two pellets in his mouth and gave Gavin the other. They munched happily through the first delicious pepperminty minutes and pulled their bogeys up the white road. Alfie's bogey had larger wheels than Gavin's and so he eagerly challenged Gavin to a race.

Gavin, a little heavier, accepted the challenge and down they flew. The small white concrete ridges of the road surfaces became a blur and the back wheels vibrated and all the loose nails and bolts rattled happily. The strings to the front wheels axle were taut and the vibrations tickled their hands. The grass at the bottom grew closer and closer, but it was Alfie who won by a good ten yards.

Below them, a hooter blew off the four o'clock shift at the tin box factory. Simultaneously, black smoke began to billow from the top of a slender tapering polyangular chimney. Soon some of the staff cars in the factory car park would slip off and join the stream in the main road at the edge of the estate.

At the top of the hill again, the two boys saw some of the lads from their school coming up a row of houses, so they steered their bogeys round and freewheeled down.

"Hiya," cried Alfie.

"Hiya! Are yer gannin' bogeying on the hill any more?" It was Dennis who ran up to meet them.

"Na. We just come doon," replied Gavin.

"Haven't y' been ter school then?"

"Na." Alfie's eyes were glinting. "Ah never dee. Ye want to come on the hill, man. Y've got it to yourself all day."

"Haven't ye been, Gavin?"

"Na. Ah've been on me bogey."

"Why, no! Y've not been in. Mr Walters noticed when he took the register."

"Ah divvn't care. He never does nothing," replied Gavin, not too confidently.

"Aye. But this time he got really mad."

Gavin made no reply.

The knot of boys began to walk up the street towards the white road. When they got to the top, a small boy ran towards them from the end of the far row of houses.

"It's Charlie Porter!" exclaimed one of the lads. "He wasn't at school this afternoon. His Mam's having a baby."

Charlie ran up breathless and red-faced. He was a smallish dirty-faced boy with a mop of yellow curls.

"She's not had it yet! The doctor's there now, an' the nurse. Me

Mam began crying out and me father told us to get out of the house or he'd thump us. So Ah come up here."

"Did the doctor use any gas? He did with my Mam," said one of the lads. "There was a terrible worry. Like, that's what Mrs Simpson said. Afterwards me Mam couldn't remember a thing. She said she slept through it all and next thing there was our Linda."

"Can Ah have a go on yer bogey, Gavin?" asked Eric Watson.

"Aye, but watch the steering."

Eric took the bogey and at the same time Alfie made his ready, and with a push off, both went skimming down the hill.

"Didn't anyone see your Linda appear then?" asked Gavin after the group had turned away from watching the flying bogeys.

"Babies divvn't just appear, y' know," said Dennis. "Sometimes they take hours to get out."

They all watched Dennis carefully. He was the one who knew all about it.

Gavin looked puzzled. "They just have to float down, man. Float down from heaven. Like, that's what me Mam says."

Dennis grinned. "Why no, man. The baby comes out of yer mother's belly. That's why she gets fat before she has it. That's the baby in her tummy."

"Ah've not seen anybody going around fat," said Gavin.

"That's why y've got a belly button. That's where y' come out of yer mother."

"It's not! It's to feed you when you're inside," snapped another boy. "Cos y're blind when y're born. Y' cannot see anything. So y've got to be fed, see?"

"Oh aye, Ah knar," said Dennis, covering up, "but supposin'-"

"Watch it ! There's Walty! Watch it! There's Mr Walters."

Behind them, striding up the street only thirty yards away, was Mr Walters. He was the deputy headmaster of Gavin's school. As soon as Gavin saw him, he began to run off down the hill.

The other boys froze. Down below, Eric and Alfie were beginning to pull their bogeys up, but they stopped when they heard Mr Walters shout. "Cooper! Gavin Cooper! Come here!

Come here at once! Do you hear, lad?!"

Gavin had not run fast enough, because in a flash Mr Walters was at his elbow.

"Now, Gavin Cooper. I've wanted to have a word with you for quite a time. Has the Attendance Officer been round at your house?" He was using the voice that he only used when he was very annoyed, and there was no kindness behind his glasses or around his thin-lipped mouth. "Well, has he?"

Gavin stood silent, slightly pale, looking down the ground.

"Cooper, I'm talking to you! Hold yourself up straight, lad!"

Slowly Gavin straightened up.

"What have you been doing today ... all day?"

"Ah had a cold," said Gavin suddenly, looking him full in the face.

"You said that only last Friday. Come on, lad. What have you been doing?"

Again there was silence. The other boys had gathered nearby and by now Eric and Alfie were behind where Gavin was standing.

"I'll tell you what you've been doing!" Mr Walters was beginning to shout. "You've been playing around the streets all day, haven't you?"

Again Gavin looked down at the white roadway.

"Haven't you?"

"Yes."

"Well, you come and see me after prayers tomorrow. You know what to expect. You're in the Easter play, aren't you?"

Gavin nodded slowly.

"Well, we'll have to see whether Miss Forster wants to keep you in the part, if you won't turn up for rehearsals. And you other boys, standing about like a load of sheep! You make sure you arrive at school prompt in the morning." Then he noticed Alfie. "And haven't I seen you somewhere before?"

"No." Alfie cheekily shook his head.

"Yes I have. I've seen you playing about on the streets before. You're at St Mark's, aren't you? With Mr Cavannah. What's your name? I bet you've been out all day, too."

Alfie was silent but beginning to look frightened.

"What's your name, lad?"

"Alfie Smith, sir."

"I'll have a word with Mr Cavannah about you. You just remember, all of you be at school tomorrow morning! You most of all, Gavin Cooper!"

Mr Walters strolled off with long paces down the hill and toward the factories. The little group joined together.

"By, Walty was mad, wasn't he?" said Dennis.

"Ah said he was, this afternoon," said Eric.

Meanwhile, Alfie was pulling faces and leering at the retreating figure. Gavin saw and joined in. Then Alfie turned to the rest. "Ah don't care. Ah'm not scared of him."

"Aye. But you should see him when he's in a temper. When he gets his strap out."

"Ah reckon you'll get the strap tomorrow," said Dennis to Gavin.

"Ah know. But it only hurts a little while afterwards." Gavin tried to sound brave. "Anyhow, I'm gannin' home for tea. Gis me bogey."

Eric handed Gavin the string and he set off down toward the row of houses.

"He'll never get any tea," grinned Dennis. "His Mam's never home."

When the five o'clock hooter went at the plastics factory, Gavin was up by the shops, sitting on his bogey, running the string backwards and forwards through his hands. Two women, shopping from the estate, came out of the Self-service. One of them wheeled a pushchair. Gavin watched them with a scrutinising gaze, and when the crowded city bus arrived and unloaded its passengers, Gavin stared at and examined each office girl, factory worker and tired woman shopper as they stepped off and made their way home.

# SEVEN

Hunter Street Primary School hall was a high, draughty and out-of-date building. Three years ago, green wash paint had replaced the thick flaking dusty cream paint on the upper walls and ceiling; only the fourth coat of paint since the hall was built in 1913. Stretching across the murky heights and supposedly maintaining the roof and walls in their present position were thick iron bars bolted together, like builder's scaffolding that someone forgot to dismantle. Falling out of the same murk were dusty maroon silk-covered wires, and at their ends, electric bulbs surrounded by wide conical pearl glass shades. At this moment they glowed a sickly yellow light.

Outside, the sun shone and it was nearly three o' clock, but inside the hall the lights had to be on. The narrow Gothic windows were high up and the sills dusty; several of the rope pulleys for opening them had snapped many years ago and still lay unnoticed and un-mended. The glass in the row of square panes of each window was so old that anyone walking along and gazing at a chimney pot outside would see it wriggle in rhythmic distortion.

Beneath the windows and running all around the hall was six foot of polished wood boarding. On these boards were green felt notice-boards displaying biblical and geography posters with rusty drawing pins. Down each side of the hall an old radiator rattled and hissed, treacherous to touch and yet with heat quite undetectable a few feet away. At the end of the hall there was a raised stage covered with tubular steel chairs and an old trestle table, all in disorder. At the sides of the stage behind the green curtains, doors led off, and on the back wall large dusty theatre flats lay stacked like pages of an old book. Either side of the stage there were double doors painted green. They led to the rest of the school.

Now the hall was silent except for the rattle and hiss of a radiator. The dust, stirred up in an earlier morning lesson, was again attempting to settle.

A small boy pushed open one of the swing doors and took half a step in, looked around and went out again, leaving the swing door shivering about its point of rest. The boy shouted, "There's nobody in yet!" and disappeared into a corridor. A few more boys mumbled a reply, footsteps and chatter started and then the three o'clock bell went. Immediately the chatter and noise grew louder. Distant slams of desk-lids could be heard, and a teacher shouting on a staircase.

Soon there was a small crowd of noisy fidgeting boys and girls waiting outside the swing doors. Miss Forster walked into the hall through the other swing doors, pausing for a moment to switch the end row of lights off and on again, in order to make the far right one light up. She looked up at the dead bulb and gave a little sigh. "Come in." She beckoned to the crowd and the children began streaming through the doors. "Hurry up and get that done and we'll be able to start."

Among the noise, chatter and clatter of the children moving the chairs, Miss Forster bent down to speak to a small pale-faced girl with her head on one side and her hair in a plait held by a red elastic band. "Yes, dear, but hurry up. You're in the first part, aren't you?"

The little girl made no reply but scampered off through the swing doors.

Miss Forster looked up at the stage and straightened her glasses. "Alright, that will be enough. Now come down here and I'll explain what we'll do. Don't jump from that stage; someone will hurt themselves, come down the steps.... Ronny, did you hear what I said?"

The children gathered round in front of their teacher and the noise and fidgeting died away. The class was completed as the pale-faced girl returned through the double doors.

Miss Foster looked around the group in front of her. "Now the bit I want to do today is where Sally and Arthur have just entered the wood and have been seen by all the animals. So I want all the animals on the stage ... not yet, just wait till I've explained. Then I want to practice the bit where the children meet Mother Spring and all the animals are hiding and watching." She looked around again and smiled. "Do you remember? Now, all the animals on the stage in their positions."

A crowd of dirty little boys and girls scrambled up onto the stage and arranged themselves in small groups.

"That's right, Peter. You look like a rabbit. Malcolm, come down a little." She stepped up onto the stage and switched the stage lamps on. For a moment the children blinked and the rest of the hall looked darker and dirtier than ever.

A little later, still in the glare of the lights, Mother Spring had moved from down the stage and towards the animals at least half a dozen times. The children playing the animals were a little tired and restless. They did not have to shout "Run! Quick! Run!" for at least another four pages.

All the children who could not read fast enough played animals because they had very little to say. Instead, they had a lot of movements to remember. This was supposed to develop their "group harmony".

Gavin was a squirrel. He was crouched near one of the long green curtains. Mother Spring moved for the eighth time. Miss Forster liked to have things right. "That's much better, Marjorie."

The bored rabbit next to Gavin surreptitiously passed him a piece of chewing gum. Gavin slipped it into his mouth. Soon the boys were chewing. Miss Forster was not looking at them as she was again attending to Mother Spring's position. Gavin whispered, nudging the lad who had given him the chewing gum and pushing him behind the dirty curtain.

"She can't see us behind here," said the lad, who was called Jimmy.

For a moment they stood rather awkwardly behind the curtain. Miss Forster stopped talking. The whole class became suddenly silent. They heard shoes come across the hard floor, and in a flash the curtain was pulled aside and she was standing before them.

"What do you think you are doing behind that curtain?!" Behind her there was a little laugh from the class. She swung round and they froze. "Well? And what are you eating? Well, Cooper?"

Gavin was silent as usual.

Jimmy spoke. "Please, Miss, he asked us to come behind the curtain to see something on the floor."

"Ah never!" burst out Gavin. "He gave us some chewing gum and pulled us."

Jimmy turned on him. "Ah never-"

"I'm not interested who did it but I can expect it from you, Cooper. You can't keep your hands out of mischief for a minute, can you? Mr Walters told me about you the other day. Take that filthy stuff out of your mouth, put it in the wastepaper basket and come and see me at the end of the lesson."

Just then the class became aware of another teacher standing in the hall and Miss Forster became aware of the class. She turned and her anger slipped into a smile. "Oh hello, Mrs Bainbridge. Have you seen much?"

"No. Only since you stopped."

Mrs Bainbridge was the Standard Three mistress and very strict, especially with the boys. If you were a girl in her class you could get away with anything, but if you were a boy....

As Gavin and Jimmy went past her to the waste-bin in the far corner of the hall, they looked straight ahead.

"They are a bad pair, those two," said Mrs Bainbridge as Miss Forster joined her on the floor. "Jimmy Wilson, he's never known how to behave himself, and Gavin Cooper...." She spoke a little lower. "Well, he's a funny boy. Sometimes he can be very cheeky. Other times, stubborn and silent. Mr Walters tells me he's a lot worse since I had him last year."

"I know, he was having a word with me just the other day." Miss Forster beckoned to Gavin. "Gavin, come here."

Gavin came and stood in front of the two teachers. The rest of the class watched, partly enjoying, partly fearing, like a crowd at the Roman arena.

"Gavin, you know that Mr Walters is not pleased with you at the moment."

Gavin knew. He had received strap. He didn't care. It hadn't hurt afterwards.

"When are you going to learn how to behave yourself?" Miss Forster began to shout, but partly to impress Mrs Bainbridge. "When you're on stage, you pay attention and wait for me to tell you what to do! Otherwise you spoil it for everyone else."

Gavin looked up at her, showing that her shouting was having no effect.

Miss Forster saw his unaffected gaze and finished off: "Alright, if you feel like that you can go. I don't want you in my play. Go on, get out and don't expect a part again."

Gavin marched off through the swing doors almost proudly. Jimmy felt fortunate to have escaped further punishment and the children on the stage relaxed again. The fury and hunger of the lions had been satisfied.

Mrs Cooper arrived back home a few minutes before Gavin. She slung her red coat on the table and slumped wearily into Mr Cooper's deep chair, eased off her high-heeled shoes, let her head fall back and closed her eyes. There was no sound in the room but her breathing and the ticking of the clock. Before the hands had spaced three minutes she opened her eyes and stared at the ceiling. A damp moistening crept around her eye-rims.

"Bugger, bugger, that's all you ever were, Harry. Bugger."

The words had come out of their own accord. Although she had spoken quietly, almost in a whisper, she suddenly sensed that it was her own voice. Realisation caused her to speak on. "I don't know why, I don't know why I ever...." She caught a movement beyond the back door and turned her head.

The door was flung open and Gavin burst in. He stopped abruptly, the wind completely taken out of his sails. "Oh, hello, Mam."

She nodded at him.

He stood uneasily.

"Well, haven't you anything to say to your Mam when you haven't seen her for five days." She fluttered a little laugh and spoke to herself again. "Eeh, five days!"

"What about?" Gavin looked puzzled.

"Don't worry, son, one day y'll understand what it's all about. Y' Dad understands. That's why he has his allotment. That's what Ah need."

"Ah gan to the allotment and help me Dad. He says one day Ah'm going to have a leek patch all of me own! Then Ah'll win all them prizes! Smashin'!"

"You do that, son. You do that."

"Aye, Ah will."

Mrs Cooper stretched out her arms and yawned but she spoke warmly. "What are we going to have for tea, then?"

"Ah divvn't know," said Gavin, still a little puzzled. Then he spoke eagerly. "Dad leaves us money for chips. Not always, like."

"He wouldn't. Not like your old Mam, eh?"

She smiled and Gavin drew away. He did not like to look at her eyes. He half ran into the hall.

She called to him from the chair, laughing to herself. "What's wrong with your old Mam? You're all Ah've got, y' know. Come on, let's have eggs for tea. You go round the shops and get a couple of eggs and Ah'll fry them. Gavin?!"

He did not reply and so she got up and went to the door. He was sitting at the bottom of the stairs.

"Will y' go to the shops for a couple of eggs for us and Ah'll fry them for tea? Will y'? What's the matter?"

"Nothing. Alright, Ah'll go."

Gavin ran off to get the eggs but when he returned he said as little as possible to his mother. Eventually they were sitting opposite each other on the table. Neither needed ask the other to pass anything. Every time his mother looked straight at him, Gavin's eyes flicked away. Now he was studying the damp swellings on the wallpaper behind.

His mother looked at the empty fireplace and shivered. "Ah think we could do with a fire in here tonight. Ah'm quite shivery."

Gavin had nothing to say.

"Are you cold, son?"

"No."

"Y' look cold."

"No."

"Are yer cold in school?" She pondered aloud to maintain the subject. "That big old school. Ah don't know how you don't all freeze to death. It must be draughty in all them corridors." For a moment she paused. "Is it draughty? Tell me, Gavin!" Her voice became more insistent, with just a trace of annoyance in it. "Tell me, Gavin, what have you been doing at school today? Say something. Don't you stop talking to me, too."

Gavin stared at his plate. "Just lessons and things," he replied slowly.

"Haven't you been doing anything special? You used to do all sorts of paintings and things."

He looked up at her face. "You've never wanted to know before. We've been doing a play. Miss Forster's the teacher. We've been doing it all term." He looked up excitedly. "Sometimes we miss sums with Mista Walters."

"You know I'm interested in what you're doing at school," she lied. "Why, only the other day Mrs Keith asked how you are getting on. And do you have a part? What do you play?"

"I played a squirrel ... like, until this afternoon."

"Oh?"

"Then the teacher tells us to go away. She doesn't want us in the play any more."

"Now why did she do that, son?"

"Cos Jimmy Wilson gives us this chewer, y' see, and she came up to us and-"

"Just for chewing chewing-gum?" Mrs Cooper became indignant. "You mean she chucked you out just for eating chewing-gum? Ah'll see about this!" She continued with a slight tenderness: "Is she always getting at you, son?"

"Nah. Not always, but there's this other teacher. She's always getting at all the lads."

"Terrifying kids. Nowadays y' can't all work well. Too frightened to speak. Ah'll go down to school tomorrow and Ah'll tell your Miss Forster a thing or two. Come on, eat up your egg. Ah'm not having them do this to my lad and that's certain."

At just about 10 o'clock, as Gavin and his mother walked up the long straight concrete path to the main door of the school, Miss Bleakley, the headmistress, and Mr Walters were talking in the office. Miss Bleakley was a small pale woman with light wispy brown hair, as yet undefined by any professional coiffure. She had small blue eyes which radiated neither cold nor warmth, and her nose was long, fine and narrow. As Mr Walters talked to her, she held her hands in front of her and rubbed them together as if at the washbasin. Her nails were square, squat and clean as a surgeon's.

Mr Walters towered over her and she only reached his shoulder. It was like that in most things. "Ah, here comes one of my most regular absentees. I wonder what Mrs Cooper will have to say. You know, his absentee slip looks like a pools coupon. Terrible little boy … funny lad."

"That's Gavin Cooper," said Miss Bleakley, getting her bearings. "Oh yes, I've run across him myself."

They both heard the school door click shut as Mrs Cooper and Gavin came in. Mrs Cooper's voice sounded hollow in the corridor. "Is this the office? Now we'll see."

Gavin made no effort to indicate that it wasn't the office and so his mother knocked. Inside, Miss Bleakley and Mr Walters looked at each other, and Mr Walter's face lit up in a mischievous smile, which was not reflected in Miss Bleakley's neutral eyes.

"Come in." Mr Walters opened the door. "Come in, Mrs Cooper. Now, is it Miss Bleakley or me that you want to see?"

"Ah want to see Miss Forster!" demanded Mrs Cooper.

"Ah, in that case you'd best see Miss Bleakley." And with a nod to the headmistress he walked out past Mrs Cooper and strolled off down the corridor, and the mischievous grin developed into a broad smile.

"Good morning, Mrs Cooper and Gavin. I don't believe I've met you before."

Gavin looked a little uneasy and stuck by his mother as Miss Bleakley beamed at them and held out a hand.

Mrs Cooper shook the hand lightly and in doing so seemed to lose some of her bluff and verbal impulse. "Gavin tells me y've chucked him out of the play. What d'y' say the teacher was?"

"Miss Forster," said Gavin quietly.

"Aye. Miss Forster. He says she is not letting him in the play. Now Ah want to know why. Gavin said he was eating a sweet or something and the next minute she threw him out."

"Well, Miss Forster is not in this morning. She is up at the William Squire School arranging scenery. So I can't get her for you. If you would like to come in tomorrow, perhaps we could clear this up. But I do feel that even if Miss Forster sent Gavin out of the class, she wouldn't have done it without a good reason."

"You call eating a sweet enough reason! You teachers always have an answer for it all! Always have an excuse for each other!"

Miss Bleakley was not to be ruffled. "Believe me, Mrs Cooper, when Miss Foster returns I'll ask her about it. But I can hardly imagine Gavin only ate sweets and nothing else. I feel it would be other things as well." She looked down her long nose at Gavin. "Was there anything else?" Gavin looked away. "Had you been naughty? Had you been fooling about?"

"You see he's nothing to say," put in Mrs Cooper. Gavin lifted up his head and stared at Miss Bleakley rather cheekily.

"Oh well, we can always find out what Miss Forster has to say."

"Aye, well, when you see her, you just tell her to put Gavin back in the play. Then Ah'll be finished."

"Ah, but Miss Forster's...." She momentarily paused. "Well, I'll see what I can do."

Just at that moment Mr Walters walked past the open door carrying some papers. Miss Bleakley called to him. "Mr Walters! Do you know anything about Gavin Cooper in Miss Forster's lesson?"

Mr Walters came in and it was obvious from his face that he had a great deal to say. "I've been wanting to meet you, Mrs Cooper."

"Oh."

The smile had gone from his face. He did not offer a hand. "Do you know where Gavin was last Tuesday?"

Mrs Cooper looked surprised and Gavin remained very still. "No. He was at school."

"Do you know where he was the Monday before, or the Friday before that?" Mr Walters raised his voice a little and pointed at Mrs Cooper with a long finger. "Well, do you?!"

"He was at school. Ah'm not going to be shouted at. Ah'm not a schoolkid."

Mr Walters seemed to have expanded suddenly, making Miss Bleakley quite unnecessary in the small room. "I'll tell you where he was. He was out in the streets playing about on a bogey! Wasting his time! Wasting ours too, and making you liable for a court case. Did you know that? If Gavin does not come to school and he is not sick, he is playing truant and that's illegal! I found him on the streets the other day and that is one of the reasons Miss Forster got rid of him. He's never there for rehearsals. You've got to start keeping an eye on him."

Mrs Cooper began to break under this onslaught. "Well, y' see, Ah have to visit my ill brother over the town, so Ah can't be here all the time."

"Aye, your brother across the town," said Mr Walters, without trying to hide his sarcasm.

"And me husband's on nights, y' know."

"Alright, Mrs Cooper, I know, but it is your responsibility to see that Gavin gets to school. We can only teach him to read and write if he gets here, and he certainly needs it."

Miss Bleakley spoke again: "Well, Mrs Cooper, I'll speak to Miss Forster about Gavin. That's all I can do."

And Mr Walters finished off: "And you tell Gavin from me, do y' hear lad, if you don't turn up for rehearsals you just don't appear in the play and that's that."

A bell rang down the green corridor.

"Alright, Gavin, you can go now, and that's all we can do at the moment. Goodbye, Mrs Cooper." Miss Bleakley held out her hand again.

Mrs Cooper shook it again, rather limply and with obvious embarrassment, but Miss Bleakley seemed satisfied.

As Mrs Cooper closed the big school door with a hollow clatter, Miss Bleakley turned to Mr Walters. "Poor woman. All that worry."

"Don't poor woman me! That woman no more goes to her sick brother than to Mecca. She spends all her time with men or playing bingo. By, I don't know what we'll have to deal with next. And that lad Gavin ... funny lad ... so sullen at times. He's no good at anything, lacks concentration. He's just led on by the others all the time, fiddling about. He has no chance in the Grading Exam. He'll go up to William Squire, just you see. He'll be in Mr Brown's class. I wonder what he'll make of him."

"I'm sure I don't know," commented Miss Bleakley, turning to her desk. The conversation was over.

Down the corridor, the school sounds settled into a quiet murmur for yet another lesson.

# EIGHT

Mr Brown moved down the row from the back of the classroom and looked over Gavin's shoulder and down at his work. "Come on, lad. That won't do. What's twenty-eight divided by four?"

Gavin's eyes focused on the paper again. There was a mass of ink blots and thin wavering lines. Down the side of the page, scrawled workings-out fought for attention with ink blots.

Mr Brown wasn't waiting all day. "Come on, lad. Come on, shake yourself. Twenty-eight divided by four...."

Gavin began to mark out little crosses in the margin.

"No, you don't do it in the margin. Your book's in a terrible state as it is. Say your four times table, come on."

Gavin began to mumble: "One four is four, two fours is eight, three fours is eight, four fours is twenty-four-"

"Four fours is what?" Mr Brown spoke without any surprise in his voice. He had been teaching at William Squire for four years now, ever since it had opened.

"Four fours is twenty-four."

Mr Brown glowered at him.

Gavin looked up and met his glower. "Please, sir."

"Now, come on. Last chance, lad. What is twenty-eight divided by four?"

"Please, sir, three fours is eight, four fours is twenty-four."

"Tell him, somebody. You, Griffiths...."

A small boy with protruding teeth and a mop of black hair stared at a massive twenty-eight dots in four lines on his page and spoke: "Please, sir. Seven, sir."

"Seven, sir," echoed Mr Brown. "Yes, seven. How many of you others have done number twenty-six on page thirty-one? Twenty-eight divided by four?"

A few boys wearily raised their right hands.

"What did you get, Thomas?"

"Please, sir. I didn't do it, sir."

"Well, you put your hand up. What did you put your hand up for if you didn't do it?"

"Please, sir, I thought...."

"Well, what did you think?"

"Please, sir. I don't know, sir." The small boy Thomas looked worried behind the thick lenses of his glasses.

"You put your hand up and you don't know why! By, I don't know what you lads'll do next." He marched down the aisle to his desk at the front. "Now everybody look at me! Johnson, at me, not your book! Now repeat after me the four times table. One four is four, two fours is eight, three fours is twelve, four fours is sixteen, five fours is twenty, six fours is twenty-four, seven fours is twenty-eight. Seven fours is ... what, Cooper?"

Gavin looked surprised. He was enjoying the table chant. "Please, sir, me, sir?"

"Yes, sir. You, sir!"

"Seven fours is...." Gavin paused and looked about for inspiration, and finally grinned stupidly like a man who knows he's bet the wrong way. "Twenty-four, sir."

"Cooper! It's twenty-eight! Remember, twenty-eight!" Mr Brown bawled. "Don't ever forget! Ever!"

"Twenty-eight, sir. No, sir." Gavin looked quite concerned.

"Write it in your books like this." Mr Brown wrote twenty-eight divided by four equals seven on the blackboard very slowly, and

Gavin copied it into his book using a spluttering school dip-pen which spat ink all around the page.

"Didn't you lads learn any tables at Hunter Street?"

Voices began to chime in from all parts of the classroom. "Yes, sir!" "Please, sir! Only up to five, sir!" "No, it wasn't, it was up to six, sir!" "Old Miss Barrett never taught us anything!"

"Quiet!"

Silence dropped like a smothering blanket, snuffling out even the most boisterous informer.

"I'm not having a noise like that when I ask a question." Mr Brown was stern. "What do you do when you want to speak to me?"

"Put your hand up," said three or four boys immediately, without raising theirs.

"That's right. Put your hand up. Don't you forget it."

Some of the boys' faces registered understanding, so Mr Brown became satisfied. "Alright then. Continue with the exercise."

For a few moments some of the class continued to stare at Mr Brown, or into, through and beyond. Heads turned idly, minds far away, until something jarred them into remembering that it was a 1B mathematics lesson. Then the heads dropped and mind and eyes re-focused on the page of division sums, pens were re-dipped in treacly ink and the next example was attempted with the usual liberal blotting.

Mr Brown seated himself at his desk, read through a little of a 1A dictation he was marking, looked up, saw that some of the class was quiet and writing, turned and looked out of the long open windows, onto the road and beyond.

Beyond consisted of some pleasant fields and a small copse up on the hill. The fields were all waving with green wheat and behind the copse rose a hill, cloaked with red house-rows and white concrete estate roads. Every few minutes cars purred up and down the road outside the school. It was not a major arterial road, but ever since the estate had pushed this far into the country beyond the suburbs, the road had inherited a stream of light traffic and an occasional but regular city bus service.

The school was lucky in being set at the edge of the country. It had its own sports fields, open playgrounds and large kitchen gardens. Other schools in the city, and even the Grammar School, came and used the athletics track in term-time for matches and training courses in the holidays. The buildings were open, square and lacking character: a glut of windows and pastel-coloured panels. A large football pitch separated the boys' William Squire from the sister girls' school, the Edith Squire. The only path that connected them was through the headmaster's garden, which was tended regularly and eagerly by senior fourth-form boys.

Mr Brown stared at the treetops of the pine copse, waving in the breeze. The same breeze pushed in through an open window at the end of the classroom and rattled an old geography poster describing rubber-growing in Malaya, ripping the second drawing-pin loose. "Put a pin in that poster, Collins, would you? There's a spare on that notice."

Collins, sitting sunning himself in the back seat, got up, turned round and re-pinned the poster.

"Thank you," said Mr Brown, almost dreamily, and then awakening a little. "Collins, come here. I've got a little job for you."

Two other boys began to mutter in the second back row. A ruler slapped on a desk.

"What's all that about?!" said Mr Brown.

Collins paused halfway down the aisle.

A boy with a dirty face and brown eyes, with a marked turn in the right one, began to speak. "It's Johnson, sir. He took me ruler."

"Ah never!" said the other boy, who must have been sweating in his woollen zipped anorak.

"Ye did. Ah saw ye," said Gavin, sounding very sure.

"Whose ruler? Come on, quickly!" Mr Brown was agitated again.

"It's mine, sir," said the boy with brown eyes.

"It's never. It's Tommy's, sir," said Gavin.

"You seem to have a lot to say, Cooper. Has this anything to do with you?"

Gavin looked a little surprised and embarrassed. He said nothing. A few boys around him began to giggle a little.

"Alright then, you two boys settle it while I speak to Collins."

A minor argument continued as Collins received his instructions. "I want you to go up to the history room and bring twenty-five modern histories down, and if Mr Albert is in there, ask him to stick all the labels in the new geography series before he uses them. Can you remember that? He knows what I mean."

"Yes, sir." Collins' blue eyes twinkled.

"Hurry along then."

As Collins opened the classroom door, the milk bell, which had just started ringing, could be heard more loudly. The class reacted immediately and sleep was cast away willingly.

"Alright, put your books away ... quietly."

Books were pushed under desk lids, some into tidiness, some into charactered disorder and some into inky messy chaos. Pens rolled down several lids and onto the floor, bending nibs and spluttering tiny droplets of ink on the green lino tiles. Eventually everybody began to settle and sat arms folded, bolt upright, like young dogs begging for table scraps.

"First row may get their milk."

Down they went to the crate by the blackboard, and hurried back to their desks.

"Second row." Mr Brown sat like a man at a control panel, and another group of boys got up to collect their milk.

"Next ... and next." The last two rows went down to the crate, and then returned to their desks.

Some boys pushed their pencils through the silver tops, punched out a tiny hole and sucked furiously. One or two used the straws which were available. Chatter and jokes sprang up and comics came out, followed by small roars of appreciation and groans of awe and despair as the metal men destroyed the bugs from Mars with an all-purging ray. One or two boys always brought out a book they were reading, a book on shark fishing or a war story, and slipped comfortably into its pages, straw in mouth, sucking gently. The talkative ones always made more of their milk-drinking than the rest, and also caused more spills and mess than anyone else.

"You'll be picking that up, I suppose," said Mr Brown, pointing to a milk-top on the floor and exercising the mild sarcasm common to nearly all teachers, whilst at the same time enjoying the hot sun at his desk.

"Yes, sir." A talkative boy ran off with the silver milk-top and dropped it with a flutter into the waste-bin in the corner.

Mr Brown always watched the boys drinking milk. What work could he do in those five minutes?

In the distance the bell jangled again.

"Alright. Pearson and Henson, you're on milk duty, aren't you? Rest of you may go."

The form trickled out, the milk monitors carried off the loaded crate, Mr Brown buckled up his briefcase, closed the door on an empty classroom and made his way to the staff room for tea and crumbly biscuits.

Outside, the boys began to invade the metalled playground. Small boys from the lower school, noisy and shrill, made contact with the tarmac and like magic began to shout and run about like whirling papers in a March gale. Older boys, usually less active, moved about in knots of two and three, slouching around the playground with an odd grunt, chuckle or guffaw. Occasionally one would slap another, the slapped would stagger back in mock pain, shouting and protesting. His friends then followed with cries and groans of sympathy and the whole capped by private jokes and insults. The games were aimless, wild and exhausting. Energies, deep and hidden completely and expertly from the master of their last lesson, were now drawn out and lost in the frenzied scramble in the yard.

Dennis had eyed a tennis ball as he dashed around the playground. He grabbed it quickly off the ground. "Hey, lads, Ah've got a ball! Ah've got the ball! Let's have a game of kingy!" He began to shout at his wheeling friends.

"Hey, Dennis's got a ball. Kingy! Kingy!"

A group was collected, formed a circle, the ball was bounced, rolled, and trickled through someone's legs. The circle exploded, order was lost and the group began again to be part of the whirling jeans and flying shoes which were all around them.

The order from the tennis ball had not escaped other eyes. The two masters on duty, balancing cups of tea and those crumbly biscuits, were moving through the square of activity like sombre monks crossing a crowded piazza.

"It's funny, you know, Jim. They only rush about like this when there's a slight breeze. When it's hot and close and there's no wind, the kids loll about and play chucks."

The science-master knew why, and started to explain.

Over by the low bicycle sheds, a group of fourth-formers were leaning on the supporting pillars and talking in the casual phrases of adolescents.

"Y' ganning, then?"

"Divvn't knar. Depends, see."

"Y' might gerrit this weekend, then?"

"Might. We're ganning to have a look Sat'day. If he's got the 350 cc, Jacky says he'll get it."

"Then we'll never see y'. Ye'll be on the bypass every night."

"Ah won't, man. Jacky'll take it with the lads. He wants ter gan fishing."

"Aye, Ah knar, with that lass of his!"

"Aye? Well? Just because ye've not got a lass-"

"Ah hev."

The others woke up at this point. Everybody began to chortle.

"Eh! Johnny Birkett's got a lass! Bloody laff!"

"Bring hor doon the Can, eh? Ah knar, it's that Sheena Price, isn't it? Eh! Sheena Price!"

"It's not bound to be Sheena Price!" protested Johnny Birkett.

"Well, who is it then?"

Johnny Birkett blushed under his dark skin. He turned at the crowd of screaming first- and second-year boys. "See that little kid

Dennis! Let's get his ball!"

They broke up and moved like lightning among the younger boys and took up position. Johnny dived for the ball and missed it.

Gavin caught it and they all pounced. He fell struggling and kicking until his clutching fingers were prised apart and the tennis ball was lost. The masters on duty had seen nothing. They were standing with their backs to the playground, admiring the headmaster's garden.

"Give us our ball back!" shouted Dennis and Gavin and the rest. They knew they had to try and get it back. For a while they chased the elder boys but with no success. Of course, the elder boys did not run about but only passed the ball among themselves, keeping it high. Suddenly a tall fair-haired boy called Jeff Peterson threw it like a bullet at Dennis.

"Here! Catch!"

Had the ball hit Dennis it would have doubled him up, but he caught it with a stinging cricketer-like slap and immediately began self-congratulation. "Hey, lads, look at that." One hand still stinging, he managed a thumbs-up.

"Quick lad, that Dennis Price," said Johnny Birkett. "Hey, Dennis!"

Dennis came running over, followed closely by Gavin, who quickly forgot his earlier pain and bent fingers as he was now in the presence of the seniors.

The seniors were fairly used to audiences from the younger classes. However, some of the more lethargic members of the senior group moved forward to impress the crowd of dirty round faces and tousled hair.

For a moment or two, Johnny looked at them all and they stared back, eager as a circus audience, and then he turned to his pals and grinned. "What d' y' think they all want?"

"Come to see ye's, man. The great Johnny Birkett!"

"Come to see me, have y's?" Johnny grinned sheepishly at the ring of seniors and lifted his arm like a parading Adonis. "Well, here Ah am ... in all me glory!"

His pals broke into chuckling and guffaws. "Eh, Johnny! Eh, Johnny lad! Parading before the littl'uns. Eh, Johnny Birkett!"

The juniors began to see that there was a joke on and some took up expressions of shy amusement.

Johnny spun around again. "What are all yous laffin' at?" And then he continued in mocking sarcasm and with a sly grin on his face: "When me and me friends have a joke, it doesn't mean all ye's lot have to join in and laff. Anyway, why are all yous lot standing around, eh?"

Dennis spoke immediately: "You called us over, Johnny."

"Aye. Ah called ye, but not all ye's lot." The crowd flinched back a little and just to help them on their way Johnny added: "Ah said Ah just wanted to see Dennis."

The cluster of boys melted and re-formed in a ring about five or six paces away.

Dennis looked straight up at Johnny's face.

"Is your dad still at the pit?" asked Johnny.

"Aye."

"So what's y's sister doing nowadays?"

"Nowt. She's ganning to the factory with the other lasses."

"Has she got a lad?"

"Nah. Not now like."

Johnny's sheepish grin returned. "Tell her Ah'll be at the Can any night, eh?"

Dennis looked away and grinned at the circle of his classmates. "Uh-huh, aye."

Johnny had noticed his grin. "And divvn't ye tell anyone, see?"

"Aye."

"And who's that lad there?" Johnny pointed at Gavin.

"That's Gavin. Gavin Cooper."

"Hey, ye's," Johnny called over to Gavin. "Aye, ye's! Come here!"

Gavin came over to Johnny and the seniors.

"See, you're on my bus, aren't you?" asked Johnny.

"Aye."

"Well, y'll be paying my full fare from now onwards. Won't yer?"

Gavin squinted up at Johnny and then he met Dennis's glance, so he nodded. "Aye."

"You don't forget what Ah said, Dennis."

Both boys looked a little uneasy and went back to their friends, who milled around them immediately.

"Tell us! Tell us! What did he say to ye?"

"What did he say, man?"

"Is it your Sheena again?"

Dennis struggled through them. "Ah'm not saying nowt."

"Na, we're not telling y's, see," echoed Gavin, proud in his new confidence.

Over the yard, the group of fourth-formers were leaning against the bicycle sheds again.

"Ah said it was Sheena Price," gibed one.

"Well, what if it is!" replied Johnny. "Some of yous buggers haven't even left y's prams yet. Ye've not had a lass in the fields, have y', Terry?"

Terry was tall and gangling with a lot of red hair and a loose drooping jaw. "Nah."

"Well, Ah have, see. Divvn't ye forget."

The whistle blew, one rippling blast. The crowd ceased all movement except for one pair of boys who continued chasing round the pillars.

"Balfour! Peters!" The science-master's voice was piercing. The boys stopped running. "What does this whistle mean?!"

To reply would mean they would have to shout, so they said nothing.

"Come and see me afterwards!" The science master put the whistle to his lips and blew a single short blast.

The frozen moment in the square became ordered movement as the boys lined up in their classes to go into the school again. A few drops of rain began to appear as spots on the hot dusty ground.

"All right, lead in."

As the last forms went in through the double doors, the rain was falling heavily and the playground was a shining black mirror. Over the hill of houses beyond, a low and heavy grey cloud filled the horizon and the house roofs became glossed. All around, the smell of cool moisture began to rise from the hot playground and followed the masters into the school to mingle with the less pleasant smells of the cloakrooms.

It was still raining when the five past four bus arrived. The sliding door opened and the mass of wet girls and boys crowded onto the steps.

"Here, here!" It was Mr Perkins, collar up and cigarette in mouth. "Let Miss Dawson through."

The crowd parted and from the back of the bus shelter emerged an attractive young teacher from the girls' school. She was wearing a fashionable sheepskin jacket and carrying a large wicker basket crammed with books and visual aids.

Mr Perkins smiled and took pleasure from her slim legs as she mounted the steps. Her champagne-coloured stiletto shoes punched little sharp stabs of sound into the steady vibrating roll of the hot bus-engine and the hiss of passing cars. After Mr Perkins had followed her, the girls and boys were even wetter, and fought it out and entered the low green bus in twos and threes.

The conductor shouted: "Come on there! One at a time!"

Mr Perkins sat down near the back with Miss Dawson. She searched for her purse amongst the visual aids, but Mr Perkins already had both their fares in his hand.

Gavin and Johnny Birkett were sitting one either side of the gangway, two seats in front of Mr Perkins. When the bus was full of noisy wet children, the folding door clashed shut and the bus started up the hill. The conductress moved up and among the row of standing children, taking fares.

"Remember, it's fourpence for me," said Johnny quietly.

"Twopenny and fourpenny," said Gavin, giving the conductress two three-penny bits.

The ticket-machine rattled and clicked out a stamped ticket. Mr Perkins noticed. Miss Dawson had not. He leaned forward. "Hey, why are you paying for both?" he said in a voice not really loud enough to be heard beyond two seats. Miss Dawson stopped searching for her purse and looked at the sly Johnny.

For a moment Gavin pretended he had not heard Mr Perkins.

"Hey, you! Yes, the little lad! Why do you pay for Birkett as well?"

Gavin reddened and lied a reply. "Ah'm not paying for both of us."

Mr Perkins ignored the lie. "Why is he paying for you, Birkett?"

Johnny turned around and looked at Mr Perkins rather sheepishly. Out of the corner of his eye he could see Miss Dawson's face watching him. "His mother always gis us his money for the bus. Usually Ah pay for him with it. She's frightened he'll loss it, y' see. Today Ah'm letting him pay, for practice, y' see."

"Come and see me tomorrow about it. After prayers." Mr Perkins did not sound very impressed. He sat back again.

Miss Dawson turned her beautiful face towards him. "Isn't that that Johnny Birkett?"

"Yes, that's right. Proper little tough man. So he thinks." Mr Perkins looked very pleased with himself.

Just in front, Johnny glowered at Gavin and the children around watched, waiting for words, but none came.

There was not even any reason for Johnny to beat Gavin up. Instead, starting the next morning and continuing for many weeks, Gavin gave Johnny sixpence to pay for their fares on the 8.40 morning bus. They were never found out because Miss Dawson, inevitably accompanied by the dutiful Mr Perkins, always caught the 8.20, as she liked to be in good time to prepare her day.

# NINE

Early in that summer of Gavin's first year at William Squire, his father fell ill with a bladder complaint. Mr Cooper told nobody, and so slight was the pain that he could hardly believe that there was anything wrong with him. Mrs Cooper, having no idea at all of her husband's illness, continued to spend much of her time away from home, looking after forgotten relatives on the other side of town, and to peroxide her hair once a fortnight.

However, one day at work, knife-edged pain jammed deep into Mr Cooper's stomach and he collapsed. Almost an hour later, over cups of tea, the works doctor told him that he probably had a small kidney-stone and was not really fit enough at present to continue his job, and that he must rest up for a while, and drink lots of water.

"How long for?" asked Mr Cooper, holding the hot mug of tea with both hands. His eyes searched the doctor's face for meaning and revelation, but the doctor had taken on an air of subtle professional neutrality. His face was friendly and almost warm, but it was giving nothing away.

The doctor, deftly holding his cup by the handle, placed it back on its saucer and said, "Perhaps a fortnight. Perhaps two or three weeks. You see, when you get to your age there are things that don't always settle themselves so easily. But if you rest up for a while and take lots of fluids, it should settle down without further treatment."

Mr Cooper looked up at the young dark-haired man in front of him, and his eyes narrowed. "So that means I'll be out of it for three weeks or so?"

"Yes. I'm afraid that's just about it."

Mr Cooper looked past the doctor and his mind tried to understand the future. Above them, in the tiny surgery, the fluorescent strip lighting seemed harsher and more artificial than ever.

When he got home it was 6 a.m. and the house was completely silent. Dawn had broken nearly one and a half hours previously, and the birds had already begun their song of the day. Cats had left the intimate confines of thick rhododendron bushes and privet; already they were waiting for the early milkman, eyes gleaming, tiny tongues licking smooth fur. Mr Cooper slipped the back-door latch, took off his boots in the kitchen and after a long heaving sigh went upstairs to bed. His wife was sleeping diagonally across the double, and so he retreated into the front room and lay down on the old single and stared into the ceiling.

He was awakened by his wife shouting at Gavin to get off to school. After a few noisy minutes, the back door slammed and he heard Gavin call someone in the street. Mrs Cooper was now in the kitchen. He slowly sat up at the edge of the bed. He did not rub his eyes. There was no real sleep. He stood up, still in his work clothes, and felt the tiny twist of pain deep in his stomach as he stretched his body. Then he went to the top of the stairs and called quietly to his wife. "Mary! Mary?!"

She came out of the kitchen and looked up at him, her hair in curlers, freshly peroxided. "Oh, have y' just come in?"

He was quite determined to tell her there and then. "Mary, Ah've something to tell you."

Slowly, step by step, he moved down the stairs, sliding his gripping hand on the banister. "Ah'm afraid Ah can't do any more work for a while. Y' see, it's me-"

"What excuse have you found this time?" His wife was not harsh, but her eyes danced with sarcasm.

"Aye, well, y' see, Ah've got a pain. They think it's me kidney."

"Why didn't you gan to a doctor before this?"

"Well, like, Ah didn't like to trouble-"

"What's to happen now, then? Ah expect y've got to gan to hospital for an operation or something?"

The sinews on Mr Cooper's hands twitched as his fingers moved backwards and forwards in nervous agitation. "No. Ah just have to rest up at home for a while. Take it easy, like." He saw the look in his wife's eyes. "Only for a while, like. Just till it wears off."

"Well, Ah'm not looking after yer and that's flat! They'll have to give y's a nurse or something!" She became more annoyed. "Who's going to earn the money?"

"There'll be my sick pay."

"Ah know. It'll be me. Ah'll be ganning out. It'll be me!"

"Ah thought we might use the holiday money."

"Aye, after saving up all year, we have to spend it all on your illnesses. First year Ah've rescued the money from being wasted on fags and seed packets for that damned allotment, and look what happens."

"Aye. Ah'm sorry, but it couldn't be helped."

"Ah'm still not looking after yer! If they say you've got to rest they should give you a nurse or something. Ah'm not giving up my few pleasures." Her manner was almost taunting. "When y' married me, you said y'd keep me."

"Aw, Mary man, don't be like that. You know Ah've always done me best."

But his wife was decided and announced with a cold precision: "Ah'm ganning out now. See how yer feel this evening." She left the house with a huge slam of the front door and did not return for six days.

As the door slammed, Mr Cooper was still standing halfway down the stairs. A few minutes later he was deep in his chair in the kitchen, smoking a cigarette and watching flies buzz around the fluff-covered lamp shade.

When Gavin returned from school he was still there. The room was thick with the smell of cigarettes and in the ashtray on the chair arm there were a couple of dozen stub ends.

"Hello, Dad."

"Hello, son."

"Haven't you been to work, then?"

"No, not today, son." He stretched himself in the chair and felt the secret pain again.

Gavin saw the pain in his father's face. "What, are you bad or something?" he asked cautiously.

"Aye, that's it, lad," Mr Cooper answered with a little sigh. "See lad, put a kettle on for some tea."

"Is Mam out?"

Mr Cooper did not answer, and so Gavin took the kettle, filled it and put it on the stove. His father watched and his eyes deepened and warmed.

"Gavin, lad...."

"Yes." Gavin turned, expecting him to say something. But there was nothing. Confusion clouded in behind his father's eyes. "Ah thought you were goin' ter say something."

Mr Cooper slipped another cigarette between his lips and lit it with a click of his lighter. His hands were shaking as he turned away and picked up an old comic. "It doesn't matter."

Gavin went upstairs to his bedroom. He took a big comic annual book from by his bed, found a blue pencil stub and began scribbling in the book. After a few moments of scribbling, he tired and just stared out of his bedroom window. Below, birds were squabbling on the wireless aerial.

It was the same each day whilst ever Mrs Cooper was not at home. Mr Cooper sat deep in his chair, smoking and drinking tea, and with the pain getting a little worse each time he shuffled off down to the corner shop for more cigarettes. Gavin spent much of his time either up in his bedroom or out for hours at a time in the fields beyond the new estate.

One day when he returned from the fields, he found the doctor and his mother and a few neighbours all round his father. Mr Cooper had collapsed again earlier that afternoon. Mrs Cooper had returned at teatime, just as the buses were crowded with factory girls and late schoolchildren. A neighbour, who came in with her, insisted on getting the doctor. The doctor told Mrs Cooper plainly, in front of her neighbours, that Mr Cooper must rest in bed and have constant attention.

Three weeks later, Mrs Cooper's hair had begun to return to its normal mousy brown colour. Her painted but uneven fingernails became cracked, dirty and roughened, and her attitude became very sour. Mr Cooper smoked less and began to take an interest in seed catalogues and gardening magazines again. Soon he was enjoying his mornings as an invalid. In the afternoons he would leave his bed and take to his chair in the kitchen.

Gavin ate and slept in the house. As the weeks went by more of his comics and his one or two books became covered in coloured pencil scrawl. Sometimes he would look at them spread out on his bed and grin. Then they would be closed and put back in the cupboard at his bedside.

Eventually the holiday money was all gone and Mrs Cooper was forced to take a part-time job. Her sourness became much less when she got a job behind the Tote at the local Greyhound Stadium. She had to work three nights a week. Now she was earning some of the money herself, she considered having her hair re-permed. Gavin watched her standing in front of the hall mirror arranging her hair into its old style. The lines by her eyes seemed deeper than ever.

"Are yer going to have it like it was, then?" he asked, looking straight up at her.

"No." She looked at him through the mirror. "One of these days, though, Ah'll gan out and have it done and then ye'll all know!" There was a hard bitterness in her voice.

"Why don't y' go now, then?"

"You haven't seen the gas-bill we got this morning. It's all them cups of tea and cooked meals for yer Dad. He's not really ill if you ask me, but he groans fine enough every time he gets up out of his bed at dinnertime. The quicker he's back in the allotment and Ah've got me house to meself, the better!"

"Aye, can we gan to the allotment soon, then?" Gavin was excited.

"The quicker the better as far as Ah care."

Mr Cooper called from upstairs. "Mary! Mary! Come up here a minute, will yer?!"

She mocked him under her breath. " 'Mary! Mary! Come and light me fag. Ah've lost me lighter.' It's always the same. Ah'll tie the bloody thing round his neck."

"Mary! It's me lighter!"

"See, what did Ah tell y'! He can't move out of his bed till after dinner. Oh no. Then he's like a cricket jumping all over the place. Alright! Ah'm coming!"

Gavin looked puzzled and then ran off to play outside, talking excitedly to himself. "Ah'm going to see the jumpy things soon! Ah'm going to see the jumpy things again!"

It was mid-afternoon. Gavin was seated high in a twisted, gnarled old hawthorn bush. It was so big as to have been more like a tree. Beneath the overhanging branches was an old ash log. It had fallen some years before, and bit by bit it had been cut back and pieces dragged away for successive bonfire nights. Now only about twenty feet of the main trunk remained, smooth yellow brown with the bark peeled off and replaced by countless initials, hearts, arrows and equal signs. Sitting on the log, and enjoying the hot wood with the countless red ants which scurried over its surface, was an old man. Patiently he filled and primed his pipe with tobacco and, cupping his thin hands over the pipe-bowl, spent three or four matches before lighting it successfully.

Up in the tree, Gavin lay across two worn-flat branches. He often sat up there, invisible, and watched people pass by on the path below. He picked a sprig of red hawthorn berries and, one at a time, began to throw them down at the old man. The man paid no attention and flicked them off like flies. The mingled smell of hawthorn bush and tobacco was delicious in the mottled light up in the tree. After a while, the man could bear the flies no longer. He took off his cap and drove them all away, mumbling under his breath.

Gavin giggled a little, then held his breath. He caught a flash of the man's fine wire-rimmed spectacles as he peered into the tree. But Gavin was no more visible than a mischievous tree spirit. The man took up his stick and hobbled off down the hard earth path.

When he had gone, Gavin bounced up and down in the branches to see how many berries he could cause to shower on the ground.

"Hold! Who is in that tree?!"

Below him stood Dennis and three other boys, with bows and arrows. Gavin froze and held his breath.

Dennis was not sure now. His dark eyes narrowed as he stared into the tree. "Ah can see you," he said, lying. "Okay men, get him down."

The three boys started forward and began to climb the tree.

Gavin immediately began to come down. "It's only me! It's me!"

"Why, it's Gavin Cooper!" said one of the boys. "You're our prisoner now."

"Leave him alone," said Dennis. "Ah didn't know ye's were coming out in these fields. Ah thought y'd be helping yer Mam as usual." He grinned a sly grin.

"Na. Sometimes Ah come out," said Gavin, sounding full of meaning and yet providing no explanation.

"Y' shouldn't sit up in trees, y' knar," said one of the boys cruelly. "Y' might fall out onto some lad with his lass!"

"Oh, but our Gavin wouldn't do anything like that, would you?" taunted the other boy.

Gavin stood for a moment, unaware of the four boys and their cruel humour. His eyes rested on the bows and arrows. "Can Ah have a game?"

"Shall we let him have a game?" asked one of the boys, turning to Dennis.

"Ah don't think he's really old enough for our games," said another.

"Aye, let him come along," said Dennis, and so Gavin followed in behind them as they padded off down the path and into the cornfield beyond.

"Let's gan to the big field," said Dennis.

Halfway down the path across the bottom of the cornfield, they cut off through the hedge of large ash trees and elderberry bushes, and into the next field. Here, tall ox-eye daisies swayed with poppies amongst the straight smooth stems of the field grass. Here and there, heart's-ease could be found, and minute insects, crawling busily around the stalks and petals. The big field was about ten acres, surrounded by a swaying wall of tall sycamores and ash trees, and had a deep dark ditch on one side. This side was always popular for playing in. Camps and forts had been built in many of the trees and old frayed brown ropes hung from the upper branches over the muddy stream. The stream often dried up and even in wet weather was only able to ooze along. Overhead, the thick foliage made a green roof to a dark tunnel. The light that filtered through was so scant that no green plants grew by the sides of the stream.

"Let's see if our old camp is still there," said Dennis to the line of boys that walked behind him.

When they got to the big sycamore by the ditch they all looked up. The rope had gone. Some of the planks had fallen into the gloomy ditch and were too soaked and muddy to use again. New branches were growing across the platform.

"Don't think anyone is using it, anyhow," said Dennis.

"Are we ganning up?" asked Gavin, looking up at the platform with excited eyes.

"Nah," said one of the boys reflectively, "someone else is going to take it over."

"To the top of the field, men!" shouted Dennis, brandishing his bow and resuming the role of leader.

They all ran up the slope to the top of the field, scattering cabbage-white butterflies and hover-flies from among the spindly long grass. As they chased their sharp shadows, they left straight tracks on the hillside behind them.

Sometimes the big lads played football on the level ground at the top of the field. Here the grass was always shorter and so it was much more difficult to lose an arrow. The target was an old tree stump, used as one of the goalposts. The boys lined themselves up about thirty yards from it and Dennis as leader made the first shot. They watched the feathered arrow disappear and reappear again just before it landed about ten feet to the left of the stump.

"Now watch me," said Barry. His arrow streaked across the field and thudded into the base of the stump. Barry's eyes glowed.

Dennis's gleamed. "Alright. See how many you can get into the stump out of three," he challenged.

"Alright. But Ah've only got two arrows."

"Well, ye'll have to gan over and get one, won't yer? Y' can't borrow mine. Y' might loss it."

Barry knew not to argue.

"Then can Ah have a shot?" asked Gavin.

"Perhaps," said Dennis, his eyes concentrating on the target as he feathered another arrow.

"Why don't you gan off home," said Barry cruelly. "Gan and help yer mother or something."

Gavin did not seem to notice. He turned to Barry. "Can Ah have a go with yours afterwards?"

Barry turned and, pushing Gavin in the chest, flung him to the ground. "Gan home, will yer!"

Gavin got up, more surprised at being knocked over than in pain. Gradually though, tears filled his eyes and he backed away. "All Ah wanted was a go with y' bow and arrow-"

"Hey, look!" said Dennis, trying to stifle his half-shout. "Behind them bushes. Lasses! Look, lasses! It's Brenda Foster. Come on, we'll surround them! Ah'll fire a shot to scare them and then we'll charge."

He loosed his arrow and it went sailing over to the girls, where they were collecting rose-hips. The arrow slapped into the ground amongst the deep grass. None of the girls noticed it.

"Alright, don't charge," said Dennis. "Drop down and crawl."

They all dropped like stones, except Gavin who first got to his knees, stared at the hedge to see where the girls were and after seeing them bent slowly forward so that he was on his hands and knees.

"Forward, men," was the whisper through the grass, but the insects paid no heed and continued to hurry on their numerous errands among the stalks. Dennis and his men crawled forward like paratroopers, bellies on the ground. Gavin followed behind them, crawling on all fours and peering over the top of the grass-heads every few yards to see that he was going in the right direction.

When they were about twenty yards from the girls, Dennis scrambled to his feet and began to run. "Charge!"

They followed him. The girls turned but did not run as the boys burst through a gap in the hedge. Instead of grabbing the girls or forming a menacing circle around them, the boys all stopped dead, just as Gavin followed them through the hedge.

Brenda's eldest sister, Janet, was with them. She was in the senior form at Edith Squire. Dennis's sister, Sheena, knew her quite well. The boys all looked a little stupid and even Gavin continued no further.

"Well, what do yous want?!" bawled a girl standing next to Brenda. She was smaller than Dennis but her frizzy backcombed hair, blown up like a golliwog in the breeze, made her look much taller.

"We was just coming over to see what ye were doing," said Dennis, looking rather foolish.

"Aye," said the girl in her hard-toned voice. "Well, now you've seen, hadaway off and play soldiers again."

All the girls looked at each other and giggled.

"Gan off and chase rabbits!" said Janet. "We divvn't like lads chasin' us in the fields."

Again the girls giggled.

"Aye, but Ah knar about you and Ronnie Wilders! You divvn't mind him in the fields, d' yer?" Dennis had dug deeply in a soft place. Gavin and the other boys grinned.

"Wait till Ah tell your Sheena about ye, Dennis Price," said Janet, obviously annoyed. "Come on, Brenda, let's gan from here and collect down in the other field." She pointed to a field which was closer to the estates.

"What about all them berries?" asked Dennis, indicating the collecting tins beside them. "Come on, men, start collecting. We'll help you get the high ones."

Janet began to move down the field. "Ah'm not staying with that lot. Are you coming, Brenda?"

Brenda did not move and watched her sister walking away. The other girls stayed with her. Janet called back, "Ah think you're crackers to stay with that lot."

Barry and the other two moved into the prickly rose bushes and began picking the orange-red rose-hips.

"Hey, where's Gavin?" said Dennis.

"He's gannin' up the hedge there."

"Shall we get him?" asked Barry.

"Nah, divvn't bother."

"What's he called?" asked one of the girls.

"Gavin Cooper," said Brenda. "Y' knar his mother's off all the time. They live in Bolton Street. His Dad's always bad, in bed."

"He's thick," said Barry.

They resumed picking at the bushes and allowed Gavin to slip away up the side of the field.

"Hey, you've got a lot!" exclaimed Dennis as he opened one of the biscuit tins. "Where'd you get them all?"

"Up in the fields, in the gorse." It was Brenda who replied. She had become the spokesman for the other girls. She had short black hair, a fine long straight nose and a pointed chin. Her eyes were always sparkling with either humour or hatred. "We're gannin' to take them to Miss Balfour."

"You in her class, then?" asked Barry.

"Yes, she is," replied one of the girls, indicating Brenda, "but her and her are in Miss Fordyce's, and Ah'm in Miss Dawson's. She's smashin'."

"What's that young teacher of yours called?" asked Brenda.

"Mr Peters?" replied Dennis, but he was not really sure.

"You know, fair hair, he gets the bus."

"Oh. Mr Perkins."

"Aye. He's smashin'. He's chasin' Miss Dawson, y' know. We asked her."

All the girls giggled.

"And she said he was always asking her out," chimed in another girl with curly ginger hair. "But she doesn't like him."

"Cos he smokes too much."

Again the girls found this a good opportunity to giggle.

"He's dead good in the gym," said Barry. "You should see him play football."

"Ah knar, we watch him through the classroom windows," said the ginger-haired girl.

"Why don't you have your hair like his?" Brenda's eyes sparkled and her mouth curled in a little smile at Dennis.

"Then she might gan with yer," giggled the ginger-haired girl.

"Who said Ah wanted ter gan with her, anyhow?" said Dennis, feeling his cheeks warming.

"We seen you looking at her," giggled the girls.

Brenda's little smile broadened and she picked up a full tin of hips. "Ah think we've got enough in here," she said.

"Would yer pay her to the pictures, then?" asked the other girl. "Ah bet yer wouldn't. Y'd only pay half."

"Ah wouldn't want to gan with ye, anyhow," said Dennis scornfully.

"Well, who's worried? Ah'm not!" replied the girl, really sounding hard enough to mean it.

"You might gan with Brenda, though?" asked the ginger-haired girl.

They all began to giggle again.

"Ah might," replied Dennis.

"An' would ye?" They were asking Barry.

"Ah might," intoned Barry, exactly as Dennis had spoken before.

"Nah. He's after you, Maureen," said the ginger-haired girl.

"Would you gan with Maureen?"

"Ah might," replied Barry.

"More than Brenda?"

"Aye. Ah might."

Brenda had collected the tins. She began to walk away into the big field.

"Where's she gannin'?" asked Barry.

They looked at her. Maureen started to follow.

"Where ye's gannin'?!" shouted Dennis.

By now she was walking deeper into the long grass of the field. "Ah'm gannin' down by the wood to the old fields. Coming?" She began to run. Maureen and the other girls began to follow her.

"Aye. Come on, lads." Dennis and Barry looked at each other but the other boy held back. "Come on, man! To the woods! To the woods! We'll catch yous!"

All three started to pursue the girls.

Gavin, high up in a sycamore, legs cramped on the tiny platform, saw them all run down the hill, saw the lads slowly catching up with the girls, and watched them pass beneath his tree and along the path until they were out of sight.

# TEN

The fine drizzle which had been falling for some time gradually turned into a soft rain, but the flames did not abate at all. In fact, it had become so hot around the edge of the fire that no rain fell on the faces of the crowded ring of children who were watching.

It had all started in the middle of the afternoon, and from the classrooms of William Squire a column of smoke could be seen over the rows of houses. At playtime, the word had gone round that it was the jam factory and that half of it was already destroyed and five fire-engines were fighting the blaze. So when four o'clock came, a stream of children from both schools descended upon the factory and soon formed into an excited and noisy crowd, three deep in many places and flickering with foolery and devilment. The firemen threw them some unfriendly looks but the children were a reasonable distance from the blazing buildings. In any case, the five units had their hands full. They had a big job on.

Flames were licking along the roof of one of the factory units, searching for anything that would burn, worrying and wandering everywhere and consuming. The hoses cast silver arcs into the fire and smoke, and steam rose from bubbling water on the twisted and red-hot roof girders. But it was too hot for the water to make much difference.

Most of the building was built of brick with a steel framework and there was little wood, but the jam and its associated products bubbled, boiled and roared into an inflammable cocktail which burned with huge luminous flames. All around there was the smell of sickly burning sugar, and the blue yellow wisps leapt greedily up amongst the spars of the roof. The paint on the spars blistered and swelled in strange disease, but the flames passed on, searching for holes and weak places, enlarging them and then roaring out of the roof in great fluttering streamers of red and yellow.

But in its essence, this was a quiet fire. Its soul and centre were subtly concealed by a searing heat and cold efficiency of flame. There were no crashes of crumbling and cracked masonry to give indication of its cause or course. Most of the buildings were single storey and only the office-block rose as a five-storeyed tower of brick and glass. As yet it was untouched, and all the firemen could do was to keep a wary eye open for stray sparks.

Half the rest of the factory was completely gutted. Part of the roof slid noiselessly to the ground, throwing up a huge cloud of sparks. The crowd of kids immediately cheered in appreciation. Faces momentarily turned to each other, revealed immense excitement and eagerly turned to face the orange glare again.

The senior fire-officer watched his teams manning the hoses, redirected another unit and under his helmet wiped his brow. Out on the main road the sodium lamps had blinked on, and in the drizzle a double avenue of haloes curved up the hillside. The grey sky was darkening, and the watching faces became more and more in highlight with flickering orange.

"Come on, you lads! Gan home now! Come on, clear off!" The fire-officer started forward and the crowd slid back a little, but at either side, sponge-like, it surged forward again. The officer nodded at one of his men, and went over to the cab of a fire-engine and spoke into the radio.

When the police van arrived, the rain was falling steadily. Many of the girls had already gone home and now groups of the boys were trickling back into the estate.

One of the policemen shouted at the ring of children. "Alright! Everyone off now! Come on! All off! It's dangerous here!"

The ring began to dissolve and reform as a definite crowd, and the crowd, amoeba-like, moved towards the double row of sodium lamps. Nearby the office-block, the policeman went to the van and took out an electric megaphone. As he spoke, the harsh tones could be heard up the hill amongst the houses. More than one back door opened and eyes peered through the grey rain at the patch of flickering golden light in the valley. But they could not see the policeman or the fire engines. That year, the November rain was living up to its reputation.

"Everyone go home now! Hurry up, please! Thank you!"

The megaphone clicked off, and another fire unit began to spray the roof of the storage building. Steam rose angrily, but gradually the water won over and began to drip and splutter onto the hot concrete floor below, passing through wisps and ribbons of sugar-laden smoke.

Back in the packing unit, rows of glass jars had turned dull-red, sagged and slipped into a pale glowing orange, becoming translucent and then opaque. Finally they flowed, fused together, and flowed on to search the nooks and crannies of the complicated machinery which until so recently had directed their existence.

A tired and sweating fireman spoke to his senior officer: "Thank God there's not much wind."

"Come on! No gassing! I want C Unit to spray the office-block. Try to keep off open windows!"

C Unit swiftly took up their new position. There was no trifling with the senior. He meant what he said.

Gavin was one of the last to leave the factory site. He had been watching lower down, by the storage unit. Then he joined in with some small lads throwing wooden stakes towards the fire. One of the firemen chased them off and Gavin retreated to watch with the main crowd.

It seemed that everyone was there. All the senior lads and some of the lasses, giggling and joking. One or two who lived further afield had cycled up and groups of seniors collected around the bicycles, excitedly arguing about the cause of the fire.

Gavin joined Dennis and Barry and a few other boys from Dennis's class. Dennis was carefully watching a group of the older lads. After a while, he left Barry and Gavin and went over to them and soon he was included in their conversation. The senior group were joined by a young man wearing a leather jacket, trousers and boots all studded from head to foot. Gavin recognised him as Johnny Birkett. He had been out of school for nearly two years now and although he never had a job for more than six weeks, he somehow managed to run a powerful motorbike. Johnny still frequented the Can, and sometimes Dennis's elder sister would return home and tell of doing 120 with him on the bypass. Johnny liked Dennis, admired his maturing craft and natural slyness, and so included him in most of his gang secrets. And his gang was an important local force.

Occasionally they would do a shoplifting raid in one of the city stores, usually on a Saturday afternoon. They would choose a book counter or the tool and hardware department, and split up. Half an hour later, they would reassemble and then go home on the bus. When they returned to the estate, they all would go to the garden hut at Johnny's and spread out the loot. This was always accompanied by a lot of argument about who had done the most daring nick. Johnny knew and respected Dennis, for he was quick as lightning at taking and concealing stuff from the shop counters. Also, Johnny could not easily forget Dennis's sister.

Now the gang followed Johnny as he wheeled his motorbike out onto the main road. Gavin and Barry saw them sliding into the grey rain.

"Ah knar where they're gannin'," Barry said, with more than a tone of bitterness in his voice.

"They'll be gannin' to dee someone in," said Gavin, grinning.

But now the gang had disappeared up the road. Red and white reflections from car lights flashed backwards and forwards on the wet tarmac.

"Nah, they're not, y' knar. Ah knar what they're gannin' to dee. They're gannin' to try an' raid the factory. Ah heard them before." Barry was excited in his knowledge, but then he became bitter again. "An' bright boy Dennis always gans with them."

"Aye. There's nee one in the factory now," said Gavin thoughtfully.

"Aye, ah knar, that's it. They'll raid it one night, take the jam and sell it all ower the place."

"Come on, you lads! Home!" A policeman had seen them loitering behind and was walking towards them.

"Stupid coppers. Aal flats are stupid," said Barry under his breath, and grinned at Gavin.

"Why are they stupid?" asked Gavin.

"Aw, come on. You're dim, just like me Mam says."

"Stupid coppers," said Gavin.

When Gavin arrived at home, there was no one in. He battered on the front door but there was no reply and so he had to walk around the row of houses and up the back lane and get in through the back door. When Mrs Cooper was away, or even just out for a few minutes, she always left the back door off the latch.

Inside the kitchen, Gavin stood for a few minutes by the dying fire, his jeans warming and beginning to steam, his eyes reflecting the magic land among the glowing coals.

A small ashtray lay in the hearth but there were only three cigarette ends in it. That meant his father had gone out to work. Since his illness, he had not been able to resume full-time work and now only went in four nights a week. When he was not at work, he spent as much time as he could in the allotment. Really there were no more jobs to do, everything was spick and span, weeds were on the retreat, but it made no difference to his fervour. Sometimes he would stare at the perfect plot for minutes at a time and then suddenly step forward with a spade and spend half the afternoon rearranging a path up by the compost heap. Often though, he could be found by his greenhouse, sitting on the crumbling green paint and woodworm of his old bench, patiently rolling and smoking cigarettes and staring across at the pigeon lofts up on the railway embankment.

Although there was no real need, Mrs Cooper continued to work at the dogs, usually for two nights a week. She appeared to enjoy the freedom and her own money, especially as her husband was no longer an invalid in bed. However, although she had more time again, she had not been away from home for several months.

When the coals had given up their deepest secrets, Gavin left the kitchen and poked his head into the sitting room. Inside, there was only the brown gloom of the settee and chairs, dull wallpaper and a dry smell of dust and furniture. Light entered the room through the lace curtains and vainly attempted to brighten the aspect. It failed in this, but it did illumine the dust-covered television with a slab of light cutting through the hanging dust. The television was surmounted by green vase full of polythene carnations.

Upstairs, Gavin slumped on his bed and heard the hiss of rain out in the darkened yards and lane. After a while, he switched on the light and then grabbed a book of aeroplanes from by his bed, but it was already scribbled in. He flicked through the pages as if examining the wild lines of blue scrawl and solemnly put it on the floor with some comics. His grin returned as he slumped on the bed again.

Next day, his mother was at home and while Gavin was out at school she decided to give his room a cleanout. When she found that nearly all the comics and books in his room were scribbled in, an instant anger took hold of her. She shouted downstairs to Mr Cooper, who was just off to the allotment. "Have you seen Gavin's books?"

"Uh?" Mr Cooper had not heard or did not want to. The garden was soft after the rain the night before and it was now ready for a good dig.

"You know that he scribbled in a few. Now they're all covered in scribble marks!"

"Well, what can yer do about it now?" Mr Cooper was dragging on his gardening boots.

"Wait till Ah see him come from school."

"Ta'ra." The door slammed.

"Ta'ra," Mrs Cooper echoed. "Y' buggers, all of ye."

All day she prepared her onslaught and as soon as Gavin arrived home, she began. "Hey Gavin, what's all this in your books?!" She waved a couple of the prime examples in his face.

Gavin grinned.

"Well, come on! Look at these!" Mrs Cooper was starting to shout again.

"Ah divvn't knar. Ah just like to go up and draw." Gavin sounded puzzled at his own behaviour. Soon he was on the point of tears.

"Aw, leave the lad alone." In the chair, Mr Cooper turned over his folded evening paper with a rustle.

"Mam, can Ah gan out now?" Gavin's face had relit. He had completely forgotten his mother's questioning.

"What you gannin' out for now? You're always gannin' out. Who yer playing with?"

"No one."

"Ah've never met anyone like him." She turned to her husband. "What do y' think? You don't just play with no one."

Mr Cooper turned out of the sports page. "What? Uh? Oh, he's a funny lad."

Mrs Cooper sighed with exasperation. "See, Gavin, you go out and play with Dennis or someone. An' don't go scribbling any more in your books! Do you hear, see you play with someone!"

Gavin ran out into the back lane.

"Ah'll have a word with that Dennis Price and ask him why he doesn't play with our Gavin."

"Oh, stop pestering the lad," was Mr Cooper's only remark.

Gavin found Dennis and Johnny and the rest of the gang up by the swings. He approached them warily. However, one of the boys standing beside Johnny's motorbike soon spotted him. "Hey, what d' ye want?"

Gavin stopped. He felt them all staring at him.

"It's that Gavin Cooper again. Stupid lad in 2C."

Johnny did not usually forget people. "Oh aye. The little lad on the bus."

Someone shouted out to him. "Hadaway, sonny, off ter y' Mam!"

"She said Ah had to seek out Dennis and play with him!" Now he was small and pathetic.

"Say, how old are you, son? Eh?" said Johnny, a little roughly.

"Ah'm twelve and a half," replied Gavin, more confidently.

"An' y' still play with Dennis?"

"Na," said Dennis, looking up at Johnny, eager to display his maturity. "He doesn't play with me."

Johnny turned to Gavin again. "Who dee yer play with, then? Eh, kidder?"

"Sometimes Ah play by myself. Sometimes Ah play with Dennis."

"He never!" snapped Dennis.

"He does sometimes, 'cause Ah've seen yer," replied Johnny. "Well, kid, what d' y' want?"

"Me Mam says Ah've got to play with Dennis."

They began to be cruel again. "Y' divvn't want to play with Dennis. He's a little hard lad. You wanter gan after the lasses. Eh, kidder?"

Before Gavin could speak, Johnny had decided. "Are yer gannin' to play with him? Eh, Dennis? Cos ye'd better gan off if y' are."

"Can't he be with us? His dad's a night-watchie at Springer's Tools."

Johnny examined Gavin's face very carefully. He reached forward and grabbed Gavin by his shirt. "See, can you keep your mouth shut?"

Gavin was in no position to do any other. "Aye." His reply was a mere whisper.

The big lads grinned and Johnny let him down. "Just remember! Say one word about tonight to anyone, and me and the lads'll do you in. And you'll be a bloody sight afterwards. You'll lose all your looks. See?"

Beside him, somebody took out a flick knife and with a threatening grin demonstrated the blade. The gang relaxed a little as they saw understanding register on Gavin's face. A big gangling lad called Bert took out a comb and began to smooth back his hair.

At first Gavin hung around outside the main knot of conversation. Dennis refused to look at him and said nothing. He was already in the inner ring of confidences, standing one hand in jeans pocket, looking as relaxed as the other lads. Soon Gavin had unconsciously imitated them, standing with all his weight on one leg, as they did. Then the group seemed to include him and he no longer stood apart from them.

He heard the big lads' conversation for the first time and his eyes widened. When he was off-guard, he would relax, then realise he was standing on both legs and suddenly move onto one again to try and regain his casual look. Eventually he ended up leaning against the wall where they were standing. One of the lads gave him a piece of chewing gum, and he heard how they planned to raid the burnt-out jam factory on Thursday night of that week. That was only two days ahead. Gavin did not annoy the big lads; in fact, they hardly noticed him, simply because he said nothing. After about half an hour's talking and joking, the group broke up. They had decided to meet again in the Can the following evening. There, they would decide the actual plan of attack.

Dennis would not go home with Gavin, so Gavin skipped merrily home by himself.

Next day, however, it was different. Dennis was suddenly much more friendly with Gavin. They bumped into each other on the way to the Can.

"What do y' think y'll have to do?" asked Gavin as they walked along.

"Ah divvn't knar. Usually Ah crawl through places where they canna get."

"What do y' think Ah'll have to dee?"

"Ah divvn't knar."

Johnny tore past on his motorbike with a leathered pillion rider.

"Smashin' bike, that," said Dennis, all aglow. "Just wait till Ah've got one."

The Billy Can was the new coffee bar up on the estate. It was between a grocer's and the Co-op chemists. After the row of shops was built with their overhanging roof, squat grey concrete pillars and flats above, the builders expected them to be taken up by firms eager for the custom on the new estates. But it was not so. The shops were taken up very slowly and there were three still empty. The Can was the most recently developed shop site.

Now, it was the centre of teenage life on the estate. Every night, groups gathered outside its fogged windows and lolled against the pillars under the overhang, and talked motorbikes, girls, boys, wages and dole. Inside, the coffee bar smelt of cheap coffee and frankfurter sausages. The juke-box jangled and thumped against one of the walls. The tables were surrounded by leathered figures and covered with dirtied scarves and crash helmets. School-kids did not usually come in unless they had a motorbike, or a friend who was working.

Gavin had never been in before, but Dennis knew it already. He pushed open the door as casually as he could. "There they are. Johnny always sits there."

They pushed through the tables toward Johnny. At first, no-one took any notice of the two younger boys. Curls of cigarette smoke rose from the centre of the table amongst the helmets.

"What d' y' bring him for?" said Johnny to Dennis.

"Ah didn't. He just come. Ah didn't, honest, Johnny. I just met him coming."

"What do you come for, kidder?" asked the boy who had drawn a flick knife the previous night.

"Ah thought we's were gan ter meet here." Gavin spoke with

unusual confidence.

"That's right, kidder. Y' remember what Ah said last neet?" Johnny's eyes were searching again.

"Aye."

"Alright. He can stay."

So Gavin and Dennis both sat down at the table.

Johnny ordered the drinks. "Hey Bert, gan and get five coffees."

Just then another of the big lads pushed through the Can door, causing the Pepsi Cola open-closed sign to swing backwards and forwards by the yellowing lace curtain. He sat down and pulled their heads towards him. "Hey lads, they's a bloody flat parading down at the factory."

"Bugger!" said Johnny. "It must be till they've got a fence round. Ah thought the coppers might stay away from this one."

Bert brought three of the coffees over. "See, someone else can go an' get the rest."

"Have you heard? They's got a flat guarding the factory."

"Y' bugger, they've been quick. What y' going to do, Johnny?"

Johnny stared into his cup thoughtfully. They all waited. "They'll be expecting lots of kids like us. First, we don't know of anyone else having a quick nick."

"Terry Marsden! He might!" said Bert.

"Nah. He's in Durham jail now."

"Aye, Ah knar. Breaking and entering!" said Dennis, airing his knowledge, but Gavin only gawped.

"So nobody will try it out, but the coppers is expecting. So let's tell them we're coming. We'll gan in by the small door at the side. It's loose cos Ah've seen it swinging. Everyone fill their bag and then out. The flat won't be around because Dennis will come running up to him and tell him that there's been a break-in of kids down at the offices. The flat'll gan round to look. He'd only be a few minutes. We can be in an' out by then. Remember, big tins of apricots. Each person take two."

"Aye."

"Do ye knar what to dee, Dennis?"

"Aye. Tell the cop they's kids breaking in at the other side."

"What am Ah ter dee?" asked Gavin.

"Ye're not in this one," said Johnny. "When we dee yer dad's factory, that's when you can help us." Johnny grinned up at the others.

"Ah would help-" Then Gavin saw Johnny's face and he stopped.

Suddenly the conversation of the big lads seemed very loud and other people could be heard for the first time. The juke-box had stopped. Johnny turned to Bert and grinned menacingly. "Put on 'When you goin' to'." It was Bert's night to pay.

The record flopped over and again the smother of fudgey sound filled the crowded room. Conversations were private and confined again. A group of people near the window got up and left. Seconds later there was a crackling roar and lights glared as their motorbikes shot off and their speedometer needles climbed and swung over and gradually slid down the other side, and steadied.

Final arrangements were made by Johnny. The time was to be nine o'clock. The place, outside the Red Gauntlet. That was quite near the factories. Gavin and Dennis got up and went off home. Johnny and his cronies were joined by some girls and conversation changed in subject, and here and there sly jokes were slipped in.

"Go and put 'When you goin' to' on again," said Johnny. Bert grinned at the girls and smoothed his hair, then he went over to the juke-box.

The sky was cold, violet, open and studded with delicate patterns of scintillating constellations and duller smudges of the Milky Way and gaseous star clusters. The moon was about three-quarters, an uneven semicircle, rising and throwing the powerful gantry crane of Weaver's Works into sharp relief.

The streets were quiet and dry. Soon a sparkling ground-frost would glimmer and twinkle with the stars. Tonight the sodium lights had no haloes; they shone at the violet with cutting intensity.

Every minute or so a car would pass along the main road, headlamps sweeping the factory walls.

Nearby the road, the factories began and stretched down the broad flat valley, now a map of pale fluorescent lights. Within, production lines continued to roll, endless belts of shaped metal pieces hanging or sitting, slowly taking on order and substance. Boiler dials were watched by old men, who consulted ancient watches and made tea, and in between read the Garth comic strip in the previous day's Daily Mirror.

The Red Gauntlet pub was quiet tonight. Outside, there was a row of parked cars. Tomorrow night, Friday, would be different. That was club night and there would be perhaps fifty or sixty cars. Tonight there was no singing, but behind the dusty coloured leaded windows someone was playing chords on a tinny piano. A small mongrel dog ran between the parked cars, across the lighted courtyard and cocked a leg at the post outside the main door and then sloped into the shadows of the pub garden. Somewhere in the factories, Gavin's father was walking down a long tool-store shed inspecting rows of coalface drills with a powerful lamp.

Gavin was squatting behind a broken and shattered field-fence opposite the car park. As he watched the dog disappear in the shadows near the lounge door, he did not notice the lads appear under the heavy telegraph pole beside the car park. Minutes later, between the wooden gaps of the fence already covered by a layer of sugary hoar, Gavin saw Johnny and two other boys appear out of the darkness up the hill.

Dennis arrived a little later and completed the group. They did not stay under the telegraph pole long, but set off towards the factories. Each was carrying a haversack. Gavin watched until they disappeared into the frost crystals and reappeared for a few seconds between the next crack, and were gone.

He stood up and immediately his face was twisted in pain. He leaned against the fence and shook his left leg. When its life returned, he set off behind the fence, hurrying until he spied the gang again. As soon as he saw them, he stopped dead and watched them climb over the fence into a field adjoining the jam factory. When they climbed the fence at the other side, Gavin was crouching ready to climb the first. He clambered over as they disappeared and ran across the starched grass. At the second fence, he crouched again and studied the group of lads as they listened to their final instructions.

Beyond them was the factory, burnt and shell-like, gaunt roof struts pointing at the stars and corrugated iron hanging heavy and loose. Part of the building and the offices over on the left were still roofed and complete. It was to the roofed part that Johnny was now pointing, for it was in there that the cans of apricots were stored.

Dennis left the huddle and slipped around the gutted part of the factory. A minute later, he returned from the other direction and whispered excitedly: "He's round at the burnt side. At the back. Ower there."

"Alreet. Y' knar what ter dee." Johnny spoke softly.

Bert and Dennis ran silently round by the gutted building to where the policeman was standing. In the still air, Gavin could hear every word that Dennis said.

"Hey, Mista. They's some lads trying to get in the office block!"

"Where, son?"

"Ower there."

The policeman began to run round to the front. Bert came bounding back waving his arms. Johnny and the rest joined him and they all made for the charred and swinging side door. Down a short corridor was the storeroom. The moon bathed all in soft blue light.

Gavin slipped down the side of the field and entered the car park in front of the office-block. At the end of the car park wall, he crashed straight into Dennis.

"Hey! What're ye deeing here?"

"Nothing," replied Gavin.

"Well, get off yem. There's a copper ower there. Hadaway, man! Ah have to gan down and warn Johnny. He's not going to be there long." And Dennis ran off around to the small side door. Already cans of apricots and peaches were being loaded into the bags.

Over by the offices, Gavin could see the policeman's torch flashing about through the windows. Back on the road he heard a car. It had become very still again. He shivered. Now he could see the torch being flashed against the burnt side of the storage unit, but the lads were safe. He was searching in the wrong part. Gavin slipped over to the offices. He flattened against the wall and edged along. Almost immediately he knocked over an empty milk bottle. The noise and the silence and the torch blinding his eyes seemed to happen all at once.

"Hey! What d'you think you're doing?! Come on, lad!"

Momentarily, Gavin looked confused and cowered a little in the glaring torchlight. Then he looked up at the policeman and said ingenuously and with a voice that suggested lines learned for a play: "They's some lads trying to get in round by the office block."

"Now look here, lad! Where?!"

"There!"

The policeman flashed the torch around the windows of the storage shed. Then from inside there came a crash and piles of cans falling.

"Aye, there," said the policeman between his teeth and he sprinted round to the storage unit. As he reached the side-door, Bert was just emerging, heavily loaded with cans. He had no time to swerve and ran slap into the policeman. Immediately, strong arms folded round him and there was no escape. The others, including Dennis, ran down the corridor and fled back into the storeroom. The policeman pushed Bert in front of him through the side door and into the corridor. From inside the storeroom came another crash and a splinter of glass as Johnny scrambled out of the high window.

Gavin saw him jump to the ground, get up and sprint across the yard to the open road. As Johnny's running steps faded into the distance, Gavin was already running as fast as he could in the other direction. He never stopped until he was safe in the long rows of old houses far away from the factories.

Meanwhile, Bert was pushed into the storeroom with the others. In the darkness, Dennis had gone very white. They could not escape as the window was too high for them and the piles of cans had collapsed. The policeman jammed the door with a charred crate placed across the corridor, and went away. They tried to free the door but it was no use. Dennis began to blubber.

"Shut up! Shut up, man! Divvn't be frightened of coppers! Y'll only get Probation."

"Aye, but-"

"Shut up! Hey, listen!"

It was the policeman returning. He had phoned from the Red Gauntlet. "Right-o, you lads, there's a car coming for you. Take you straight to the best beds you ever been in." He heard Dennis blubbering. "Aye, you need blubber, lad. But y'll do more than blubber when we've finished with you."

Twenty minutes later, all the lads were safely secured in the local police station. Later in Court, no one dare split on Johnny. Bert and two others with previous offences were sent to Approved School and Dennis was put on Probation for a year.

As soon as Mrs Cooper heard that Dennis Price had been put on Probation, there was no doubt at all in her mind. Gavin must never play with Dennis again. Gavin smiled foolishly and nodded, and his mother took this as a token of obedience. She would always be ignorant of the fact that Dennis had decided never to say another word to Gavin and that he encouraged his friends to do the same, and as they did not share his natural malice, they taunted and tortured Gavin instead.

And so as Dennis was coming up to be a leader and people were taking notice of him, Gavin was drawing closer and deeper into worlds within himself.

# ELEVEN

In the William Squire staffroom, masters were sitting deep in soft armchairs, clustered around the gas fire. By their sides were cups of tea, precariously placed on the thick pile rug. Balanced on the saucers were biscuits, crumbling biscuits. It was lunchtime, and half of the staff was away dealing with the first sitting of lunch. The rest were sitting and drinking their tea and trying to relax. The games-master might have been in with them but he was out taking cricket practice. The pleasant woody click of cricket bat and ball drifted across the field and through the large open glass windows.

The staffroom was at ground level. Outside was the head-master's garden. Leading into the garden was a slim glass door. Beyond the garden there was a low wall and beyond that the Edith Squire staffroom. The buildings of the two schools were mirror images, but that was perhaps as far as the comparison went.

On the staffroom walls were wild mosaic paintings and an abstract ceramic mural, all products of the fertile mind of the art-master and his classes. Just now he sat hunched up behind a Daily Sketch. Although the lines in his face might have revealed something of his age, there was no grey in his short black hair.

As often happened, he began to shake with laughter. "Hey, William! Look at this." He passed the paper over to the geography-master, who was marking exercise books piled on his knee.

"What?"

"That, man. The joke at the bottom corner. Eeh, man, I'll die in a minute." The art-master collapsed back into his chair, helpless with laughter.

The geography-master searched for the joke, surveyed it for a few seconds and exploded into laughter. "Hey, fellahs! Look at this!"

The paper was passed around the remaining masters and each time, it produced grunts and laughter. Even dry Mr Ramsay, the metalwork-master, was able to raise a wry smile.

"You know, I think his jokes are getting better every week," said the geography-master. He turned back to his marking and silence fell over the staff again. Someone stirred his tea and with a clink replaced the spoon on the saucer.

Mr Webb, the history-master, came through the French window. From his face, the rest of the staff knew that the lunch was as unexciting as ever. Mr Webb stretched himself by the window and watched the cricketers coming from across the field. "Oh, thank God! Only two more weeks!"

"Come on, Mr Webb! That's not the way at all!" Mr Priest, the maths-master, spoke mockingly, using someone else's words, hot and cosy in his armchair. "You have fourteen more days with 2B. Use them wisely. No day at school is ever wasted." The other staff members grinned. They recognised the source of those words of wisdom and advice.

"Load of little buggers. That's what they are," reflected Mr Webb, still staring out of the window.

"Hey, Arthur, look at this!" The geography-master passed one of his exercise books to the art-master.

"Oh aye, I get this in art, too." He chuckled. "At least it's not always misused energy there."

"What's that, then?" asked Mr Priest.

"Gavin Cooper in 2C. Look." The art-master held up the book. The blue scrawls could be plainly seen by everyone.

"Do you know what he said to me the other day in history?" Mr Webb started another one of his stories. "He started to do all his scrawling, aye, and it's always in blue, and I said to him: 'What's that, man?' I tell you I nearly died. He said: 'It's me map, sir.' I said: 'That a map of Roman Britain?' He looks up at me and says, 'Yes, sir.' He doesn't bat an eye. Funny little lad."

"Well, I'm not having it in my books," said the geography-master. "Look at that. Terrible mess."

Again they looked at it.

"I think the lad's screwy, y' know," said the art-master, lighting a cigarette. "Want one, William?"

"Aye, I will. Thanks, Arthur."

"You should see some of the rubbish he comes out with in art."

"Well, he can't read, can hardly write his name. And mathematics! He needs personal coaching all the time."

Gavin's tired form-master looked up from a pile of reports. He pulled Gavin's report out of the pile. "Just look at his report! Eight subjects. Two 'Below Averages' and six 'Well Below Averages'. He's a harmless enough lad, but I would never give him any jobs to do. He cannot remember a thing. Really, I don't think he ought to be here. He ought to be over at High Hills."

The geography-master grinned broadly. "If I had my way, I'd put half the little buggers in there. Hell, man, there must be a dozen like him in the school. Nicholson in 1B for a start. He's a stupid lad. And that Neville Parker. No relation of yours, eh, Jim?!"

Mr Parker tapped ash off his cigarette in the saucer. "No, William, I won't sue you this time."

"Actually...." Gavin's form-master was hesitant. "Actually, I was going to mention it to Allan. I mean Cooper having a test."

The art-master shook his head. "Malcolm, I tell you. The lad's not got a chance."

"Well, I think he might have a go all the same. He might do much better at High Hills."

Mr Ramsay turned to them from his chair. "He'll be wanting a job in less than eighteen months. He hasn't a cat's chance in hell of being anything but a labourer. Do you know, his dad once told me he wants Gavin to be a turner at Springer Tools. Most parents just don't seem to realise."

"Allan's on duty with me today. I'll have a word with him then."

At half past one, Malcolm Wilde went down into the yard and blew the whistle. Lunchtime was over again. Allan Barclay, the second-year senior master, came over to him as he stood in the middle of the yard. Mr Barclay always seemed to wobble on his short legs.

"Thank you for bringing them in, Mr Wilde." Mr Barclay smiled and, deep in his face, his eyes twinkled.

"Oh, that's okay," replied Malcolm, conscious of the other's seniority. "Mr Barclay, I wonder if I might have a word with you about Gavin Cooper in my class."

Mr Barclay's twinkle disappeared. His serious let's-get-down-to-business face appeared. A face which many a new boy had learned to respect in double-quick time. "Oh, yes. He's the slow boy, isn't he?"

"Yes. Well, I wondered if he might have a test for High Hills? His work is very poor, yet he's harmless enough. No real trouble in the class."

Over by the school, the lines were filing into the changing-room hall. Mr Barclay looked keenly at Malcolm Wilde. "Do you mean that you, as Cooper's form-master, are formally recommending the lad has a test?"

"Yes."

"Alright. I'll speak to the boss about it after the kids are in." He glanced down at his watch nestling in long black hairs. "I'm free now. You realise he has no chance of getting in. They're packed out up there."

"Well, I can do no more."

"No, that's true."

They turned and went into the school, Mr Wilde to Gavin's class and Mr Barclay up to the headmaster's office.

Wilfred Manners was a headmaster with no particular streak of administrative genius and no stream of revolutionary ideas about teaching methods. What he did have was an even temperament, a level-headed approach to his many problems, a cool courage in carrying things out in the face of a reactionary, somnolent and uneducated Education Committee, and above all, the respect of everyone on the staff.

When Mr Barclay knocked at his door, he was sitting behind his huge oak table-desk working through a pile of senior reports. Sun blazed into the room and lit up the photographs of the past three years' senior cricket teams and an inter-town swimming shield the school had won the previous year. He did not look up. "Come in."

Allan Barclay put his head round the door.

"Oh, hello, Allan. Come in. I'm very pleased with this 3A lot. Ten of them wanting to do O Levels in four subjects. You must have really shaken some of them up."

"Yes, they did have a Barclay pep-talk late last term."

"Good. It's the only way for the brighter ones. Now, what can I do for you?"

Mr Barclay wasted no time. "Malcolm Wilde would like Gavin Cooper in his class to have a test for High Hills. Really, I think the lad ought to go there as well. And by the way, you know Malcolm's wife is just about to have their second child?"

"Good. Yes, I know about it. We can let him off to go off to the hospital, as I can cover if necessary. He's a good man. And I'm pleased that Mr Wilde has picked Cooper out. I've been wondering what to do about him for some time now. The lad seems way behind the others in most things."

"You agree, then?"

"Oh yes, I agree, but it'll be a hard job to get him in. You know what they're like up there. I'll write a note for his parents this afternoon. We must waste no time. It's near enough at the end of term. I suppose he might get in for the next year."

"Alright then, I'll drop in and see Mr Wilde."

"No, don't bother, Allan. I'll see him, and Cooper."

Later that afternoon, just before playtime, Mr Manners knocked and entered the 2C classroom. Some of the boys shuffled to their feet, but Mr Manners waved them down. As he spoke to Malcolm Wilde, the bell went.

"Alright! Books away! Leave quietly! And Cooper, would you stay behind a minute? Rest of you, out!"

The desks and room emptied, and Gavin came over to Mr Manners. Mr Manners waited until Gavin had straightened up, then he smiled a little. "Mr Wilde and I want you to give this note to your mother or father as soon as you get in. Can you remember to do that?"

"Just for me?"

Mr Manners looked at Mr Wilde and their eyes met in understanding.

"Yes, there's only one," said Mr Manners in a helpful voice, "so don't lose it. Give it straight to your mother when you get in. You'd be better collecting this from Mr Wilde at four o'clock. Let's see. You do take 2C then? Yes. So get this from Mr Wilde at the end of school. Alright. You can go now."

As Gavin left, Mr Wilde collected together books off his desk and put them into his briefcase.

Mr Manners spoke again: "He has no idea at all, has he? Just tagging along all the time. You can see it in his face. Still, he might make it."

It wasn't until Gavin was out walking down by the old Jubilee Pit that he remembered the note. He pulled the letter from his shirt and ran home, with the sun sinking and the evening shift starting at the mine.

When Mrs Cooper read it, she was amazed and immediately indignant. "They want our Gavin to have a test or something. They say he is 'not responding to their form of teaching and that he might ...' " she paused, " '... benefit from the smaller specialised classes at High Hills.' Our Gavin is not going up there. There's nothing wrong with him. Once y've been in there, no one speaks to you." She looked at Gavin, who was standing by the table. "Have you been messing about at school? Ah'm not going up there to fight all your battles for you. Look at this." She read again from the letter. " 'Perhaps you would like to come and discuss the matter with Gavin's form-master, Mr Wilde, and myself. Yours sincerely'... ugh! Why can't they just teach you up there? Why do they make all this fuss? Anyhow, Ah've changed my mind. If that's what they want, Ah'll go and see them and Ah'll tell them. There's nothing wrong with our Gavin, is there, son?"

Gavin smiled a little stupidly and then dropped his head and studied the tablecloth pattern.

Mr Cooper turned from his chair. He had just arranged the letter in his mind. "You go up and see them, Mary, if yer want. But Ah don't know what all their fussing is about this time."

Next morning, Mrs Cooper entered the side gate and marched through the headmaster's garden, with Gavin following behind.

Watching from his study, Wilfred Manners turned to Allan Barclay. "Some of them will never learn the proper entrance to the school, even after four years."

Mr Barclay's eyes twinkled. "You're lucky she's come. When he was marked absent this morning, I thought she was going to keep him for the rest of the term."

"Ah, well. Prepare for battle."

There was a knock on the door.

"Allan, could you go along to 2C and get Mr Wilde and sit with the form. It may be some time." He winked. "Come in."

Mrs Cooper, wearing a blue coat and a brown patterned head-scarf, pushed Gavin in front of her and entered the room. Mr Barclay glanced at Gavin and left the room without a word.

Mr Manners smiled pleasantly. "Come in, Mrs Cooper, and sit down. Gavin can run along to his class now."

"He's not leaving me," she said flatly. "It's about him Ah've come and he'll stay."

"Yes, that's just it, Mrs Cooper. There's no need for Gavin to hear all I want to say. I would prefer him to run along to his classroom."

"But he's staying with me!" Mrs Cooper was not giving up any ground. She sat down and Gavin stood beside her.

Just then there was a quiet knock at the door and Mr Wilde entered. His thin white face and fine features looked more drawn than ever.

"Oh, come in, Mr Wilde. Have you had any news yet?"

Mr Wilde shook his head slowly. "No. Maybe it should be Friday. Maybe tomorrow."

"Good. And remember you can slip off this afternoon any time. Just let me know." Mr Manners returned to Mrs Cooper. "Have you met Mr Wilde, Gavin's form-master?"

Mrs Cooper had turned her head and now she nodded from behind the headscarf.

"Sit down, Mr Wilde. Mrs Cooper would prefer Gavin to remain here whilst we discuss...."

"Oh...." Mr Wilde inclined towards Mrs Cooper. "I don't really feel there is any point in letting Gavin hear all I am going to say. I would feel much happier if Gavin were in his class getting on with his lessons."

Mr Manners concurred. "You see, Mrs Cooper, there are one or two technical things which don't refer to Gavin personally. To keep him here, we are just wasting his time."

Suddenly she relaxed. "Oh, alright, he can go."

Gavin got up and moved towards the door.

"And mind you keep out of mischief!" she bawled after him as he shut the door.

Mr Manners glanced at Mr Wilde, but Mr Wilde was not looking. "Yes, well ... this is simply the position, Mrs Cooper. Gavin is in 2C. That is the lowest stream in his year. Many of the children in it can hardly read or write. Because of staffing, there are thirty-nine children in the form and many of them will never read or write properly. Some of these boys are badly behaved and lazy. That's one reason why they do not learn well. Gavin is not one of those boys. He is neither lazy nor particularly badly behaved. In fact, he is quite a quiet boy. Yet he does not learn well. In fact, he is falling behind the others in the class. Mr Wilde and Gavin's other teachers believe this is because Gavin is not really suited to our kind of teaching. He needs a smaller class where he can have more individual attention and special help."

"Well, he's not going to High Hills and that's that." Mrs Cooper was stubborn again. "Gavin isn't ill. He's not mental. That's what High Hills is for, and Ah know. And he's not going."

Mr Wilde leaned forward again. "Really, Mrs Cooper, you've got it all wrong. High Hills isn't a lunatic asylum. It's a special school for children who aren't really suited to normal education." He appealed to her: "They get on much better there, believe me."

"And so our Gavin isn't fitted for here, then?" said Mrs Cooper, giving the words a harsh ring.

"No, quite honestly, he's not," replied Mr Manners calmly from across the table. "He is lagging behind now. In eighteen months, he'll be looking for a job. At his present rate of learning, no one will want to give him any job at all. At High Hills he can be taught a particular skill and be prepared for a job. They can concentrate on his strong points."

"Aye, but from what you say he doesn't seem to have any."

"Nearly everyone can be useful in some small way or another," replied Mr Manners, really doubting whether what he was saying was true.

Mr Wilde took up the thread again. "You see, Mrs Cooper, Gavin has problems with his concentration and possibly some ability, but he channels all his energy into scribbling in his books and tearing up papers into squares. Up at High Hills he could be taught to use these energies usefully."

"Aye, well, he's pencilled in all his books at home, too. Made an awful mess of them."

"Well, there you are then," slipped in Mr Manners. "Why don't you let him have the chance for individual help from High Hills? He would go on the school bus. There'd be no fares. Let him try the test."

"How long would he be there, then?" Mrs Cooper sounded a little more interested.

"He'd go, just like our school, every day, until he became fitted for this school again. Then, all being well, he would return here." Mr Manners reached for a pen on his desk. "So will you agree to Gavin having a test, then?"

For a moment, she sat still as stone.

"Believe me, he will benefit. What it amounts to is VIP treatment from the Education Authority. They can do no more to help him. So can he have a test?"

"Aye, well, Ah suppose so. If you think it's best."

"Well, I do," said Mr Wilde.

"And so do I," agreed Mr Manners. "I'll write a note about fixing the time, and let you know immediately." He wrote a few notes on the pad in front of him. "Alright then, Mrs Cooper." He stood up and smiled. "I don't think you'll regret it. The boy could really benefit."

She got up and turned to go.

"Goodbye, Mrs Cooper." Mr Manners held out his hand.

Mrs Cooper took it uneasily. "Goodbye, sir." She spoke quietly and hurried from the room.

When she had walked across the headmaster's garden and passed through the side gate, Mr Manners turned to his colleague. "Really, you know, it's dreadful. She was quite frightened at the end. I think their own schooldays come back to them."

"Either that, or common sense. She'll probably change her mind before lunch."

But Mrs Cooper did not change her mind. She felt uneasy about the whole business of High Hills and told no one but her husband. Mr Cooper took little interest. It was exactly one year since his kidney trouble and he sat on his chair continually expecting some sort of dreadful resumption of the illness. This gave him a good excuse to stay in his chair and not strain himself.

After the actual day of the anniversary had passed and nothing happened, Mr Cooper was almost a little annoyed. However, he stuck to his chair and cigarettes, deciding another week was necessary before the threat of a relapse could safely be said to have passed. His wife took no notice of her husband, but when it was fine outside she encouraged him in a not very subtle way to get off down to the allotment and see to his leeks. Invariably, Mr Cooper realised that he wasn't wanted and shuffled off to put his allotment boots on.

On the Wednesday of Mr Cooper's extra week of medical precaution, the letter arrived about Gavin's assessment interview for High Hills. Mr Cooper opened it and passed it to his wife. Mrs Cooper read and understood it and at half past three the next afternoon she took Gavin up to High Hills School. She had peroxided her hair especially for the occasion and Gavin wore a new pair of shoes. However, neither mother or son showed any other signs of preparation.

In the main building of the school, they were ushered by a passing teacher into a small waiting room with two glass doors. Hardly had they sat down when a young secretary opened the door on their left. "Mrs Cooper?"

"Yes."

"Would you like to come this way, please? And Gavin, stay there. Someone will come along and collect you in a minute."

Mrs Cooper obediently passed into the office beyond as the secretary held open the door. In the office, a kindly-looking fresh-faced man rose from behind a table. He nodded to the secretary. "Thank you, Mabel."

The door closed with a heavy click as the secretary disappeared behind the rippled glass.

"Please sit down, Mrs Cooper."

She sat down. Her bleached hair poked out through her brown headscarf. Her large shiny black patent-leather handbag lay on her knees.

"We shan't keep you long. Just basically a few particulars to check off. Mr Manners has sent me most of what I want to know in the way of dates, ages, addresses and so on. What I should like to ask you is one or two questions about Gavin himself."

She nodded.

"You see, if we find that he needs to come here, we like to know as much about him as we can before he arrives. Then we can save time and it makes it so much easier for his teachers. If we know him 'inside out', so to speak, then we can really begin bringing the best out in him." He looked at his pad. "Now, does he sleep well?"

"Oh yes."

"Does he have nightmares and so on?"

"No. He's never been that sort."

"Does he eat well?"

"Oh yes. He eats nearly everything Ah give him."

"Do you think he's a happy boy?"

"He always seems happy to me."

"I see. And does he have many friends?"

"Well, he used to go around with a gang of lads. But now he doesn't play with them."

"Why not?"

"Well, Ah told him not to. They were in Court with the police. So I told our Gavin to keep away."

"So he plays by himself now?"

"Yes. Now."

"And have you seen or noticed any change in him? Over the last six months?"

"No, Ah don't think so. Y'see, Ah'm out quite a lot and me husband's on nights. Ah don't see all that much of Gavin."

"I understand what you mean." He would have liked to have smiled to himself, but his job did not allow him to. He continued asking questions and taking further details from Mrs Cooper, while in an airy room down the corridor a young specialist teacher was watching every move that Gavin made in a series of assessment tests.

"Now, Gavin," the young lady teacher smiled enthusiastically. "I am going to tell you a true story about a couple of sailors in the war.

Afterwards, you tell me what you make of it, okay?"

"Yes, miss."

Almost an hour and a half later, leaving behind them two piles of foolscap sheets covered in new information, Mrs Cooper and Gavin were re-united in the waiting room. The secretary saw them out of the school and soon they were at the bus stop.

"What did she tell you a story about, then?" asked Mrs Cooper.

"Some sailors and a submarine," replied Gavin, not very enthusiastically.

"What did they do, then?"

"They went and sunk a submarine."

"Oh, I see. What else did she say?"

"She gi's all these pictures to look at. Ah had to choose. She asked us about our holidays."

"There they are, prying again. These teachers can't keep their noses out of anything. And what did you say?"

"Ah said we never had any. And me dad was ill. And she asked us about the allotment. She said her dad once tried to grow leeks, but he couldn't. That's because he didn't knar me dad's secret."

"Was she nice, then?"

"Just like a teacher. Alreet. And she was writing down all the time. But her dad didn't know my dad's secret, did he? That's why he couldn't grow his leeks."

"I suppose so, son." Mrs Cooper seemed none the wiser. Then the bus came and they got on and returned home.

Mr Manners saw the letter from High Hills almost as soon as he entered his office. He hung up his coat, sat down and for a moment stared at the envelope. Then he picked it up, slit it open and read the letter carefully. "Oh hell. Just as I expected." He sighed.

After prayers, he showed the letter to Mr Wilde and Allan Barclay. They stood in the library. A form, sitting in the library doing a reading duty, eyed them curiously from behind their coloured sports-books and encyclopaedias.

"See? What did I say?" said Mr Barclay.

"Well, we tried. It's all we could do. Heaven only knows what'll happen to the lad now, though." Mr Wilde, now looking much less haggard, would be slipping off to the hospital in the evening to visit his wife and his new daughter.

Mr Manners read from the letter: "'We do not really consider that Cooper can really be classed as ESN. We recognise him as a difficult case, but we do not really believe that he would benefit from a period of education at High Hills'. They just don't like teaching kids who won't give them positive results. I don't know....'"

"Well, that's that. It's always the same," said Mr Barclay. "What'll that mother of his say? That's what I'd like to know."

The letter fell on the doormat by the second post and no one was in. Just before lunch, however, Mrs Cooper returned, and after making herself a bit of lunch she went upstairs. As she came down again, she spied the letter. She ripped it open clumsily and unfolded the crisp typing paper.

She read it through once and then again. "See what Ah said. I knew them masters were all wrong. There's nothing wrong with our Gavin. Just like a blooming hospital up there anyway."

Mr Cooper came in from the backyard, carrying a bag of potatoes.

She heard him close the back door. "Is that you?" No answer. "Make sure you take them boots off!" She went into the kitchen. "They don't want our Gavin at High Hills. They say there's nothing wrong with him, just like Ah said. Those masters don't know our Gavin like Ah do. They only teach him. The letter says he should remain at the William Squire School."

Mr Cooper dragged off his boots. Mud from the potato patch pattered onto the carpet. He wriggled his grey-socked toes and began to feel them again. He sighed. "By, Ah need a new pair of boots. These'ud strangle yer if y' stayed in them long enough."

"Do you hear that about our Gavin?"

"Oh aye. But Ah don't know what all the fuss is about. Gavin's alright in the allotment. One day Ah'm goin' to give him my leek recipe."

"Aye, an' that'll be all," said Mrs Cooper under her breath.

He turned to her. "What?"

"Oh, nothing." She went into the hall.

Gavin did not arrive home until nearly half past six. On the side of his forehead was a smudgy blue mark.

"Where've you been?" asked his mother. "Have you been fighting?"

"Up in the fields. Ah've been up in the fields."

"What've y' been doing up there?"

"Jus' playin'."

"Oh. Anyway.... Well, you're not going to that school up on the hill. We had a letter. You're staying at William Squire."

"Ah never wanted to go anyhow. All the lads say they're all thick up there. So Ah'm not going."

"How did the lads know you were going?" Mrs Cooper sounded more concerned than usual.

"Leslie Scott saw us gerroff the bus."

"But shouldn't he be at school?"

"Nah, he's absent."

"By, Ah divvn't know what these schools are coming to!" said Mrs Cooper.

Gavin left the room and went upstairs. And that night he scribbled in the three new comic books. Then he was satisfied and fell asleep easily.

# TWELVE

Every day the sun climbed higher into the sky and in the early afternoon, as gangs of men were slipping out of pubs to start the afternoon's work, the road surfaces and hard white pavement slabs grew hotter and hotter. On days with no cloud, pavements became so hot in the close rows of houses that spilt ice cream and lollies from the ice-cream man dried and hardened in minutes.

Lucky children, unable yet to walk in the spring, now dribbled their orange lollies down their chins and daubed their little white jackets, toddling and staggering about in tiny runs of satisfied balance. They grinned and gurgled at their mothers and brothers and fell onto their little cushioned behinds and kicked bare and grimy feet into the air. The glass in the gutter always seemed to be a measured distance from where they fell.

Later, flies settled on the cast-away damp lolly sticks. The children ran into the dark cool insides of the houses, yelling for sweeties. A cat on the coal-house roof stretched itself on the hot concrete slab, where it had remained unnoticed for nearly an hour. People never seemed to look upwards. Over by the coal-house, a pile of damp wood had become dried out for the first time in the year. Orange maggot eggs, sticking to the wood like barnacles, were slowly being burned lifeless. Other insects and crawling things had left the tangle of split wood for the darker, cooler, moister confines of the coalhouse. Perhaps there they would bring forth new life amongst the pile of old gardening magazines.

After a few days, the roadmen left the street, taking with them their monster tar boiler, their red lamps, halt signs, braziers and the dusty frayed ropes. But when the sun rose higher at midday, the new tar began to run and bubble, and soon a crowd of little boys in Palmer Street were running from one section of mended road to another, popping the tar bubbles. After an hour of this, much of the workmen's labour seemed to be transferred to the boys' hands, but what did it matter, the ice cream man was coming to the street in a few minutes. They rushed indoors, crying, "Mam! Mam! It's the icey! It's the icey! Mam!" or bawled through the letterboxes, "Mam! Can Ah have an ice?"

Some of the mothers met in the sun, one wearing a scarf on her hair, with a pale face and sunken eyes, and nicotine stains on her fingers. She exchanged a few words and a joke with the Italian ice cream man (born in South Shields), laughed a little and then broke into a deep rustling cough, put the back of her hand to her mouth, stepped back and turned to a neighbour, still laughing. Beside her, a small round-faced girl wearing a smudgy bonnet and a dirtied blue dress lifted tiny hands and bright eyes for her ice cream.

Gradually these hot and happy days passed and the sun occupied less of each day and the late-night sunsets sank back into the evenings. The evening dew that made a pearl out of each polished car became earlier and heavier, and the leaves on the trees looked soaked and tired, flowers became berries and soon autumn was only a few weeks off.

It had been a good summer and up at the Burnside Farm, just visible from some William Squire classrooms, Mr Barker sat in his farm kitchen and looked as pleased as he would be all year.

The following January, his lease would expire and his land and house were to disappear in a new high tide of estate development. The kids had already broken his footbridge hand-rail over the burn

for the third year running. Gradually, their cycle tracks and play
areas and temporary football pitches in his fields had been wearing
the land away from him, but soon it was to be really theirs, and the
burn a fine new sewer. His cornfields were interlaced with patterns
of flattened crop: the kids again. But there was no doubt about it,
this last summer had been good for Burnside Farm and Mr Barker
reflected it in his satisfaction.

At the edge of one of his cornfields, staring into the trickling
waters of the ditch, sat Gavin. In his mouth was a length of sweet
grass stem. Around him were split blades of various grasses. He
had been trying to make a whistle, but seemed to have forgotten
how to hold it between his fingers. He tossed the last grass blade
into the air and watched it flutter and settle on some thistles
nearby. Then he settled back and his eyes examined the hedge on
the other side of the stream.

It was a hawthorn hedge, not very well-kept, and numerous gaps
were present along its length. Spiky hawthorn branches stuck out
at all angles and helped to cover the stump of an old oak tree. It was
about eight feet high and had been sawn down many years before.

The upper part of its wide bole seemed a good place to sit. Gavin
eyed it with immense satisfaction, as if discovering it for the first
time. A few noisy chattering hedge-sparrows fluttered in branches
that had sprung from the edges of the felled tree, but ceased their
squabbling and took to the air in a blur of wings as Gavin sprang
across the ditch and landed beneath the stump with a thud. He
scrambled to his feet and squinted up at the new and hidden
resting-place.

Two minutes later, he was sitting high up on the tree stump. In
nearby bushes, some of the sparrows watched him nervously. He
parted the surrounding oak branches. Beneath him, on the other
side of the hedgerow, was a track leading to a road beyond and in
the other direction to the Jubilee Pit. Before him, on the other side
of the path, lay a field of turnips.

Already the shadows of the hedge and the oak stump cut sharply across the path, and the dried cracked earth was cooling rapidly. Beneath the sun, the horizon was becoming hazy. It was not too late, however, for a butterfly to flutter about and across the turnip field.

Coming down the path from the Jubilee Pit were two boys. One was wearing a dark suit and had metal-rimmed glasses, the other a grammar school blazer. Both had their hands deep in their pockets and were engaged in quiet conversation. They were aware of nothing outside their discussion. Gavin watched them closely and grinned at their pressed trousers, school ties and short haircuts.

As he watched the two boys, a group on cycles came clattering down the path behind them. Gavin immediately recognised Dennis and four of his gang on track-bikes. For some weeks they had been converting old scrap racing-bikes. They had turned the drop handlebars upside down and made sure at least one brake worked. Then they were able to use these bikes to dash around the estate and along the cinder tracks. In a few months they would all want, and eventually get, motorbikes. The hillocks of the old Jubilee slag heap had been a good place for practising dirt track and daredevil riding.

And now they were chasing up the path behind the grammar school boys. As they passed and the two boys stepped aside, one of the gang shouted an insult. Just below Gavin, Dennis screeched to a halt and collided with another bike. There was a crafty glint in his eye. Gavin watched, fascinated. He could have called out but then he would have given away his newly-found hiding-place. So he stayed silent.

For a moment Dennis looked at the grammar school boys. "Hey, did y' see that? One of them buggers up the path stuck his big arm out and tried to knock us off me bike! Did y' see?"

"Aye, Ah saw," said Barry.

The others nodded, knowing what was coming.

"Just hold me bike, then," grinned Dennis. There was a relish in his voice. "While Ah gan and beat his bloody face in."

He called out to the approaching boys: "Hey, ye big buggers!

Which of y's tried to knock me off?"

The two boys looked up but continued to walk on. Just as it seemed that they were going to walk right past the gang, Dennis sprang forward, white-faced. "Hey, yer bastards. Where y' think ye're ganning?" He grabbed one of the boys by the sleeve of his blazer.

The two boys stared at him, surprise and fear dancing in their eyes. "We were just walking down the path." The boy in the blazer spoke in an accentless voice, but his face betrayed his anxiety. His spindly companion blinked slightly behind thick-lensed glasses.

"Oh, do you hear that, chaps?!" Dennis swung round to the gang, mocking the grammar school boy. "I say, we were just walking down the path."

The lads gathered round with a mocking laugh and a few remarks such as "jolly hockey sticks" and "well, I say".

"Oh, so you was walking down the path, was you?" Dennis had returned to his normal voice.

"Yes, we were," replied the grammar school boy. The other continued blinking. A ray of the setting sun sparkled on his metal-rimmed glasses.

"D' y' hear that, lads?" Barry leered. "Two lads walking alone in the fields."

Dennis and the others grinned and chuckled.

"Bloody poofs! That's what yous are." Barry pointed his finger into the boy's face. "D' y' hear that? Bloody poofs. What are ye's?"

The grammar school boy stood silent and unflinching. Inside his trousers, his legs began to shake.

"What are ye? Ah asked ye a question. Divvn't cheek me, son, eh?!" Barry grabbed hold of the grammar school boy by the lapels of his blazer and held him close to his roughened red skin and long greased brown hair. "What are ye, son?" he breathed. "Eh?"

"Leave him alone a minute," Dennis interrupted. "We divvn't want to fright the bastard, do we now?"

"Bloody poof!" rejoined another of the gang.

Dennis smiled and nodded his head slowly, then he turned his white face to the two boys. "One of yous two tried to shove me off my bike."

"Why would we?" started the grammar school boy with the blazer, but Dennis's angry face and blazing eyes prevented him from saying any more.

"One of yous stuck his bloody arm out as we passed and tried to knock me off me bike. Ah just want to know which it is. Then Ah can flatten his heed."

"I'm sure my friend here wouldn't want to do anything like that, and I know I wouldn't."

"Look! One of yous did. All Ah want to know is who did it, then Ah can thump him up."

"Bloody poofs!" Barry stepped up to the fair-haired boy wearing glasses, and put his face as close as he could. "What are ye? Poof! Can't ye speak for yerself, eh?"

The boy stood blinking and swayed back a little. "I have nothing to say. I know none of you."

The gang burst out into mocking guffaws and an almost chilling hysterical laughter. All except Dennis, who continued to gaze at the boys with his cold angry eyes. For some reason he was in a white rage.

"Hey, Dennis man! He has nothing to say!" shouted Barry.

Dennis looked closely at the thin pale bespectacled face and smooth chin, and said quietly, "He did it. Ah remember now."

"Aye." The other members of Dennis's gang immediately agreed.

"I'm sure my friend-"

"Shurrup, ye!" yelled Barry.

"He did it!" said Dennis more vehemently. "Bloody poof! Take y' glasses off and Ah'll thump y's up!"

But neither of the boys moved.

"Yer bugger! He's bloody dumb or something," Dennis shouted. "Can you hear me, son?!"

"I can hear you perfectly, thank you," returned the quiet

accentless voice in the blazer.

But Dennis was concentrating on the other boy. "Well, are yer going to take y' glasses off? Eh?"

The pale face turned away and faced the haze that was growing around the red orb of the sun.

Barry tried to attract his attention. "Hey, specs! Poof!"

"Aw, leave him, Barry, man! He's a stupid poof." Dennis approached the boy with the blazer. "Will yer fight for y' mate, then?"

"No. I have nothing to fight about. I have no quarrel with you. I know neither my friend nor I attempted to knock you off your bike."

"See, kidder!" Barry advanced, undoing his thick studded belt. He ran the belt through his fingers. "You'd better make your mind up. Are yer fighting for your mate?"

"No." The grammar school boy added quietly: "What for?"

"Just a bloody poof, aren't you?!"

The grammar school boy looked around at the leering faces. "Because I know the rest of you will join in. I don't want to be hacked to bits and left in the ditch."

Again the gang growled and chuckled in cruel guffaws. Dennis lost some of his rage. "See, kidder! Where d' y' live?"

"In Thrunton."

"Do yer live in one of them private houses?"

"Yes. What is wrong in living in a private house?"

"Ah bet yer dad's never done a day's work in his life, has he?!"

"See, kidder...." Another of the gang advanced up to the boy's face. He took out a long bladed knife and grinned menacingly. "Why do you need to wear creases in yer pants?" He jerked the knife forward. "Eh?"

"I have to wear them. I've always worn them. It's part of my uniform."

"Errr, lads! It's part of my uniform!" This was too much for Barry. "Poof! Yer want to wear jeans like we dee!"

"Which school d' ye gan to then? The grammar school?"

"Yes. So what?"

"All the poofs gan there," said Barry.

Dennis inclined his head towards the pale-faced boy in the dark suit who was still watching the hazy sun sink into the cornfield. "Does he gan, too?"

"Yes."

"Is he a poof?"

"No."

"He is, yer knar," said Barry, grinning and prodding the grammar school boy in the chest. "Isn't he?!"

"No, he is not!"

Barry did not move but continued to leer up at the boy, and for a moment took on the outline of a foul and grotesque mediaeval hunchback. "See, Ah bet you never been with a lass."

The boy remained silent.

"Have yer been out with a lass?"

"Nah. Course he hasn't! Bloody poof!"

"Let him answer." Dennis grinned again. "Let him answer."

But there was no answer.

"Haven't ye been on the nest? Eh, son?"

"Na," said another of the gang. "He wouldn't knar what ter dee."

"Ah knar," chuckled Barry. "Ah dee."

"Dirty bugger, ye!" said Dennis, turning to him and grinning. He returned to the grammar school boys. "What d' ye dee at night then, if y' divvn't chase lasses?"

"He gans for walks in the fields," Barry collapsed into horrible laughter, "with his friend."

But the boy was saying no more.

"Ye working for exams, then?"

"Yes."

"Are ye?" Someone prodded the boy with glasses and then pulled all the pens out of his front pocket.

The boy was standing there serenely, staring at the dimming sun, seeming almost asleep on his feet. But then he spoke. "Yes."

Barry jumped into the air. "Err, lads! It speaks! It speaks!"

By now the pens and biros were being taken to bits and the bits dropped into the deep grass by the path.

"Hey, come on, lads! Let them alone! What about the lasses down at the swings?" One of the gang was tiring. "Aw, come on, Dennis, man. Let's leave these poofs be by themselves."

Now each pen was scattered about the grass at the side of the path and only a smudge of orange pink remained on the horizon where the sun had set.

"Alreet, lads! Howay then!" Dennis ran over and picked up his bicycle. "And divvn't you poofs ever forget. Divvn't try to knock people off their bikes."

They all mounted their gaudily painted track bikes and clattered off down the path.

The grammar school boys collected themselves.

"Hell, Peter, you said a lot, didn't you?" said the boy in the blazer.

The other boy had taken off his spectacles and was using his handkerchief to polish the condensation from the lenses. "They've gone now," was his only remark.

"Here's some of your pens. Come on, you find them too! Don't just stand there. It's actually a good thing you said virtually nothing. One wrong word and we'd have been in little bits by now."

"So you see yourself as the fearless emissary to the savages, then?"

"Oh, shut up! I was scared stiff."

"I told you we shouldn't have gone for a walk."

"You know, Peter, it's about time you saw the real world." The boy in the blazer spoke sarcastically. " 'Get on the nest', and the rest of it!"

"Come on, I've got all my pens now. You are welcome to continue your insults when we get out of these fields."

As the pale pink haze in the western sky sank lower and lower and was overcome by a bank of dark grey cloud which slowly crept up and over the sky, the two boys set off down the path. After a few yards, the boy with the spectacles replaced his hands in his pockets.

Before they were out of sight, Gavin clambered down out of the tree and jumped onto the cracked earth of the track. He watched the boys turn off the path and onto the road.

"Bloody poofs!" he chuckled to himself. "Get back ter where y' come from."

He bounced off along the path and then, finding another gap, cleared the ditch again and rolled over into the stiff yellow-brown corn. For a few feet he crawled through, pressing down the stalks with his hands, slinking along like a tiger in a bamboo thicket. There was no grass growing on the dry grey soil around the bases of the corn stalks. A red brown dust fell from the ears above and powdered his hands and hair.

He knelt and looked across the top of the corn for quite some time. The heads swayed and rustled and shook their loosening grains. Ahead, the sky was dark and louring. It seemed that the clouds were being exuded from the open horizon line on the top of the hill. Above his head the cloud became closer and greyer and diffused and mingled with the pale haze of blue of the sky in the east. Over the next few minutes, the delicate blue of day slowly disappeared into the unfathomed and colder violet of dusk.

A breath of cool wind slipped across the rustling corn heads and reached Gavin. He shivered. The wind swept through him again, and once again. Each time, his body was seized with a shuddering and paroxysmal shiver. Suddenly the cornfield had lost its warmth and protection, and before the wind came again Gavin was up and off, running toward the road as fast as he could go.

The corn slashed and beat against his legs; twice he stumbled but he ran on, leaving behind him a new trail of flattened crop. At the fence he clambered over, crossed the road, ran through the next field and reached one of the streets on the edge of the estate.

Once on the hard white paving stones, Gavin stopped running and began to amble and dawdle along, trailing the back of his toe in the gutter, driving forward a little pile of dust and matchsticks until they fell through a drain grid. Round the first street-corner, opposite a grassy square across from which a new primary school was being built, his scraping toe collected an old sardine tin. But he did not kick it, only trailed it on until it slipped past his foot and was left behind.

Now his arms were limp by his sides, as if he had nowhere to place them. Normally his arms would have been live and tensed, sensitive to every movement, helping him to keep a perfect balance, but for some reason they hung useless and he stumbled when his left foot caught on the edge of a badly-fitting paving-stone.

Not only had life left his arms. His face was dulled. There was no sparkle in his eyes, no movement in his lips. His hair had fallen forward and he stared at the ground in front of him, sullen and disinterested.

Ahead of him, an iron garden gate clanged shut and a tiny child ran out onto the pavement, screaming. It clutched its hand and howled, red-faced, round-mouthed. It turned a tear-stained face to a window as a figure within knocked on the glass and beckoned. Behind, there was a silver glimmer of a television.

Gavin passed the child and never looked, seemed not even to hear. The people behind the window saw him pass but did not notice him.

He crossed the untidy worn grass of the square. In the middle was an old iron bedspread and mattress. The mattress was split and leaking feathers, which in the hot weather had blown all about, becoming caught in the privet hedges and on the piles of rough earth around the new school. But Gavin's eyes never left the ground. He trudged on heavily, bearing an invisible burden.

A big moth slipped and fluttered into the street from out of a hidden vegetable patch and passed close by Gavin. For a moment he watched it. Then he seemed to reflect and become alight with its movements. His face lit up and he reached out and followed the beautiful delicate brown insect as it wandered through the air. He raised his arms and cupped his hands to catch it, but missed; then ran forward a little, and jumped and missed again. But soon the moth had disappeared over a tall garden hedge and Gavin was left alone again. Slowly he let his raised arms fall limply by his sides and as before, his movements became dulled. The excitement drained from his face and his expression became heavily set and clay-like.

Beyond the square was the children's playground. There were swings and simple roundabouts. Over in one corner was an old steamroller, firmly cemented to the ground, and beside it two sections of large white concrete pipes, end on end, separated by a crack just big enough to squeeze through. Gavin had no interest in the empty swings and went straight over and sat inside one of the pipes. The air was much cooler now the sun had gone in, but here it had become very close.

Gavin looked up at the sky through the crack separating the pipes. A great dark cloud had covered the whole sky and all the colours of the sunset had been squeezed away. Now the clouds seem poised over the earth itself, ready to begin to press down and choke. It was quite dark, and the mercury street lamps began to flicker on.

Suddenly, down in the street there was a shout and a peal of laughter. "Eee, Leslie! Divvn't dee that. Ah'll lose all me chips, man!"

It was a girl's voice, and as Gavin scanned the playground from inside his pipe, Dennis and the gang and some lasses appeared as they mounted the playground steps. They had returned from the chip shop in the next street.

"Gisuh a chip, somebody! Hey, ye, Nancy! Gisuh a chip!" It was Leslie Scott, taunting one of the girls. "Hey, Dennis! Where d' y' say these lasses come from?"

The girl screamed and giggled as he made after her again. "What's your name, girlie? Eh?"

She stood facing him a few feet away, ready to run.

"June." Her voice was low as she spoke, and immediately she giggled at the others.

"Well, Ah want some of y's chips," grinned Leslie.

"Aye, Ah knar!" she giggled. Her brown hair fell in front of her face. He rushed at her again and she ran screaming and giggling down past the roundabouts.

"It's ye he's after!" yelled Barry.

Before his words had died away there were large spots of rain appearing on the dry concrete by the pipe. Over by the houses, Gavin caught a glimpse of a soft grey curtain advancing as fast as a man could run and with a quiet hiss, turning to a roar as the rain and hailstones reached him. All the ground was immediately wetted and glistening. The hailstones bounced into the pipe and Gavin moved away from the crack.

All around the roar of the rain pelted and drummed on countless tin roofs of garages and sheds. He heard another shout and a clatter of feet. "Up here, man!"

Through the crack between the pipes, Gavin could see Leslie climbing up the side of the steamroller and the dark-haired girl scrambling up behind him. "It's shelter," shouted the boy above the rain, and looking up at the old cab roof.

Lower down, the girl had less cover. He urged her to climb higher. "Come on, man. Up here."

"Ah canna. There isn't room." She strained upwards and her heels slipped out of her shoes.

" 'Course there is," he shouted, pulling her further up, and she clung to him for balance and tossed back her soaked hair and laughed with him.

Between the pipe and the roller, the rain beat down on the grey concrete, forming a thick carpet of splashed spray and vapour. Drips began to run along the inside of the pipe and drop on Gavin's neck. He edged back a bit.

But he still watched the girl and the boy as they laughed and shouted in the rain. He could see the pink of the girl's limbs and the pale flowered pattern of her soaked dress clinging to her body. He could see the bunched and quivering muscles of the boy's arm holding them both up against the roller, and the light blue of his jeans becoming darker and darker as the water crept through them.

"Ah know!" the girl cried. She laughed and sprang away from Leslie and, kicking off her shoes, ran barefoot across the carpet of spray to the end of the pipe.

From the gloom within, Gavin only caught a glimpse of her face and streaming hair as she crouched in the entrance before he scrambled to his feet and ran from the other end of the pipe towards the gleaming and motionless roundabouts.

He heard no shouts as he cleft the silver grey curtains of pelting rain and reached the top of the playground steps. Already he was soaked to the skin, and the hailstones lodged in his hair and stung his face, but he felt no wet at all. It would be some time before the soft cooling of the rain would soak into his hot and glowing body. The blood was singing in his ears and behind his eyes his heart beat faster and faster. But now his legs were running down the steps and his body and arms were balancing him. His face had lit up in an expression of irrepressible joy. His muscles were tense and sure. He had become alive.

He ran lightly along the street and took a running jump at a large puddle. As he landed, he let out a nervous high-pitched laugh. The splash sent flashing tongues of silver all around him, but he paid them no heed and only ran on.

The rain was dribbling down the gritty walls of the coalhouse, seeping into the cracks and soaking the pile of wood. Fibres, baked dry, were beginning to twist and swell. Dehydrated maggots' eggs, already dead and almost dust, were washed away to rot on the dirty concrete slabs in the yard. Long-legged spiders made a hurried dash for cover but were caught and drowned, pressed hard to the ground by hailstones and huge drops of rain. Gutters struggled and drainpipes tinkled in strange music as an inch of water found its way into the ground. In the square, the old bedstead prepared for rust and the mattress lay soaked, limp and exhausted, the feathers grounded.

Out in the fields, the earthy path had become pitted with drop marks and would turn to mud when next walked on. The ditch was beginning to fill up and become alive again, and the brown water deepened in colour and carried scraps of grass and cardboard and debris down to the burn.

When the rain was over and the ground was sucking up the precious gift, Mr Barker stared out at his darkened fields and heard the rushing torrent of the burn next to the farmhouse, and turned away from the window. His summer was over.

# THIRTEEN

The year became evening and in the shops, Christmas cards and gifts and new trends and fare were piled high in the windows, inviting people to buy. And even though many had barely recovered from their holidays, they bought the gifts and followed the trends and wore many of them out long before Christmas truly arrived.

And as people were returning from late holidays and the worn grimy posters in the railway stations were replaced with scenes of mountains and snow, chalets and return-fare charges, the trees in the city parks were tiring and the leaves were weakening on their stems and turning yellow. The grass in the fields was old and greying, and the berries on the hawthorn bushes had loosened and fallen. Filled with sweet and ripe crop, the fields of turnips were nearly ready for harvest, but the corn had gone. Much had rotted on the ground, and with no real regrets Mr Barker had gone too.

Autumn had truly replaced summer, but that year it was hardly a real autumn. The russet and wrinkled leaves never really hung whispering and fluttering before a light breeze. They were never whirled from the bending trees and dashed against buildings and hedges like grains of flying sand. There was no fluid carpet of yellows and rust curling and spinning down the paths in the park and amongst the trees. Instead, the rain dashed the weaker leaves to the ground where they fell heavily. The rain held them to the ground and soaked them and rotted them. And as they began to dry out and lift from the paths in the wisps of wind, it rained again.

That year there was no late season of sun and scudding clouds and bracing wind. It rained often and piteously into the season of frosts, and the matted leaves were carried into drains and later sworn at by Irish labourers who shovelled them into lorries and scraped them out of drained paddling pools.

In the streets, people began to wear the plastic macs they had almost dared to forget about in the long summer. Gay umbrellas bounced and swayed above the crowded pavements of the city rush-hour. Above, the neon signs and strip lighting glowed in the growing darkness and reflected on the wet streets. And at the bus-stops, workmen with plaster and mud on their trousers scanned the racing results in the evening paper, and rows of young shop-girls linked arms and chatted and giggled all along the crowded pavements and watched boys from the engineering works who sheltered in doorways, smoking and holding their haversacks and planning their evenings. And little fat women, round-faced and deep-eyed, complained about the bus services, the weather, the prices in the shops, and clutched bulging paper carrier-bags which only made them look ridiculous and more obese.

Out in the road, the dripping cars crawled past. Fords, Vauxhalls, Austins, a Jaguar, two vans filled with estate workmen, and at last the bus they were all waiting for, almost full. The little fat women pressed forward, crowded aboard and squeezed into seats and arranged their carrier-bags. And upstairs, there was a blue haze of Woodbines, threads of smoke running along the yellowed paintwork of the roof all covered in condensation. When the bus left the centre and the shops and came into the suburbs, the estates were wet and the streets were empty. People hurried from the bus through the rain to their firesides.

But in mid-November the rain turned to mist and fog, frosts crispened the air and people went out into the streets again and visited friends, went to dances, and the kids went to the Can and sped their motorbikes on the bypass and the air cut sharp and painful on their faces.

Sometimes on those wintry evenings, Gavin would watch them flash past from behind the frosted windows of a lonely bus bay. Sometimes he would even go down to the Can and watch the motorbikes and gangs and their lasses laughing around the squat pillars. But he never crossed the road and spoke to them. He would hang about in the shadows, his face concentrating on their every movement and his ear tuned to their every sound. He would just stare and stare until someone looked his way. Perhaps they had seen the vapour of his breath reflected in the sodium lamps. But hardly had they begun to tell their pals, when he was gone. He slid into the shadows and up a dark back lane behind a row of small flats. But he had stopped running home and instead he would turn in the safety of the darkness and face the activity, lights and noise of the coffee bar and stare again.

Gavin seemed to like the dark nights. He could observe and watch the world and not be seen. He could slip into the shadows and disappear. He never went into the fields now. They were brown and bare and the hedges were spiky and hollow. The trees offered no cover and it was cold sitting cramped up in the branches. There was no light to see anything by, except in a full moon, and usually the mists made that valueless. So Gavin had turned to the streets, followed the lights, and where there were lights there were people and where there were people he watched them.

In early December, Mrs Cooper discovered that no more books or comics had been covered in scrawl. Gavin spent little time in his bedroom now. He was out so often. When he came in, he always said he had been out with the lads and Mrs Cooper was satisfied, but the lads never called for him. But then it had always been like that. No one had ever called for Gavin.

Sometimes after school was finished, Gavin would hurry down to the electronics factory entrance and stand waiting for a bus home. At 4.30 p.m. the bell rang shrilly, once, and immediately the staff began to pour through the gate. Some of the men rode out on bikes, but not many. The bus service was far too good and it was worth a long journey to keep a job on the trading estate these days. All day the factory girls had sat at long conveyor-belts surrounded by wires and instruments, assembling the intricate printed circuit transistors. And now they ran across the main road in chatting groups of two and three and made a long queue at the bus stop. Some had umbrellas and many wore flat shoes and carried deep wicker baskets. Some had prepared for an evening out. They had their hair done up in curlers hidden behind headscarves. They all seemed to have little chunky red legs and round wide-eyed faces, and a few had tinted hair brushed back, coarse as fuse-wire. And they chatted and giggled in the queue and Gavin watched them, but they never noticed him because they were too busy discussing their own worlds. One day, many of them would be little and fat, waiting for the bus and clutching their carrier-bags.

Not every evening was spent around the factory or down at the Can. Gavin had found the working-men's club and discovered the resident singer. She was slim and blonde and worn, but her lips were red and her teeth flashed and her eyes sparkled in the stage lights. Clutching the stick microphone in one hand and using the other to etch her song into the air, she intoned her ballads with the electronic organ until the clapping began. And Gavin watched her from outside, his face pressed close to the window glass and condensation. No one ever saw him because they were too busy with their talk and beer, and when she had finished her songs he usually went away.

At weekends his activities were different. There was no cloak of darkness, so Gavin stayed in the house on Saturday mornings. In the afternoon he would go down to the allotment with his father and dig and weed. Mr Cooper was surprised at his eagerness, especially on Sunday mornings when Gavin used to ask if he could go down to the allotment again and dig, have a fire, or tidy up the compost heap.

But as dusk fell on the winter afternoons, Gavin's enthusiasm for digging waned and before Mr Cooper had looked up twice, the spade was back in the shed and Gavin was off up the path, home for tea.

After Christmas had gone and the New Year was firmly established, everyone expected snow but none really came. There were only two or three days of wet sleet, and soon people began to feel the first pangs of spring in the air. After a little rain in early February, everything became warm and moist and new growth began to show on the trees and flowers. Some people began to spring-clean, and the family next door to the Coopers got a housing transfer for a new flat on the estate and were soon gone.

Now there was lots of work to do in the allotment and as the evenings began to brighten, Gavin often went and tended his own patch of garden. He planted some lettuces, and at last the day came when his father gave him a leek plant of his own. Eagerly Gavin transplanted it, but somehow it did not seem to thrive as it had done before. Mr Cooper had still not told him his secret recipe and so each day it looked worse when Gavin came down and watered it.

One late afternoon, as the sun was fast slipping below the pigeon lofts on the railway embankment and the pale shadows of the sheds and fences lay across the narrow paths of the gardens, Gavin stood by his leek plant with a watering can in his hand. Behind him, coming down the track, were two girls from St Mary's school, the local Roman Catholic secondary modern. One of the girls had fair hair and was carrying a beret and on it was the large silver cross of the school badge. The other girl was taller and dark-haired. Clasped in her hand she had a coiled dog-lead, and behind her a small corgi sniffed and searched in the grass and bounded here and there over the track. The girls were talking quietly, and their casual shoes crunched on the coke and cinders.

Gavin heard them when they were still some distance off and immediately he turned round and watched them. The watering can still hung emptied from his hand.

The girls did not appear to notice him as he stood staring from the garden. As they walked past and the dog sniffed and poked around the fences, Gavin's head slowly turned and his eyes followed. The girls disappeared behind a long row of greenhouses, and only then did Gavin turn away and a quiet smile flickered on his lips and his eyes were lost in fantasy.

Behind the greenhouses the girls began to giggle.

"He didn't care, did he?" said the dark-haired girl.

"Na! Ah thought he was gan ter ask us in!"

"Ter help with the weeding?!"

"Something like that."

They looked at each other and giggled again. Soon they were doubled up with laughter.

"Ah thought he looked alright. For a lad, like!"

"Really, Margaret!" said the fair girl.

"Divvn't, man! Yer sound just like Sister Stevens."

They walked to the gate in silence. Then the fair-haired girl made up her mind. She held the gate open. "Ah wouldn't gan out wi' him."

"Eh, Janey! Ye're still thinking about that lad in the allotment."

After that, Gavin began to go down to the allotment every day, and the girls made the allotment track one of their regular walks through the dark. Each day the girls passed, Gavin would stand and watch them, and out of the corners of their eyes the girls examined his standing figure and saw the hazed grey sun light up his staring face. This went on for four days, but on the fifth day the allotment gate was not safe in its sneck and it swung a few inches ajar, and the sniffing scurrying corgi dog easily nosed its way through the gate and up by the greenhouse.

Gavin did not notice the dog at all. He stared straight at the girls but they would not turn their heads to look at him directly. When they were almost past the allotment, Margaret remembered the coiled dog-lead in her hand and turned and looked for her corgi.

"Where's Corky? Corky! Corky!"

But the dog did not heed her. He was busy digging and worrying in Mr Cooper's prize leek patch. Then Gavin saw the dog and the flying soil, and he ran forward.

"Hey! Gerroff, dog! Me Dad's leeks! Gerroff!" He swung his shoe at the dog, who stared up at him cheekily. Then it bounded away up to the compost heap, bending another leek plant as it jumped.

Margaret and the fair-haired girl came into the garden. She called the dog: "Corky! Corky! Here, boy! Come on, boy!"

The dog scuttled down the path into her outstretched arms and quickly she fastened his lead.

Gavin was gazing at her widely-spaced eyes and her dark hair at the sides of her face. Then she lifted up her head and patted the dog's sleek and quivering coat. For a moment their eyes met.

"Has he done any harm, then?" she asked.

Gavin turned sharply from her stare. A vague flush crept up his neck.

"Nah. Well, it's me Dad's leeks." He seemed to stand helpless.

"Let's see, then," said Margaret.

"Does y' Dad pay y' for workin' in his garden?" asked the fair-haired girl. "We seen you here often."

"Nah."

"Will yer be working in here every afternoon, like?"

"Aye. Well, there's always stuff to do. Me Dad's always planting stuff and we have lettuces and taties later. When they grow up."

"Oh, Ah see," the girl answered, soft and neutral. Then she began a new tack. "D' ye knar Len Hargreaves, Danny Walters and them lads?"

"Nah."

"Ah wish we did," sighed the fair-haired girl.

"Which school do ye gan tee then?" asked Margaret.

"William Squire." Gavin answered automatically and he pointed to where he thought the school was.

"Oh, them lads all gan to St Paul's." Margaret patted the dog, who was straining on the lead. "Can Ah have a look at yer leeks, then?"

Gavin's eyes lit up. "Aye, if yer want."

He led them to the leek patch where the couple of dozen or so big green plants grew in solitude and had individual attention.

Margaret started forward. "See, he's knocked this one over. Look, it's all split here. We'll put it up again for yer."

"Aye, ye'd better. If me Dad sees that...."

The girls crouched down on the dry ground and began to pack the grey soil around the base of the injured plants. Corky pulled the lead from Margaret's hand and as the dog moved away, the shining leather slipping across the dry soil like a lazy snake, Gavin saw Margaret's bitten fingernails and stumpy fingers and the nape of her neck, white-skinned where her long dark brown hair had fallen forward. He glanced at Janey's short fair hair as she squatted down beside Margaret, but his attention was not held for long. Soon he was studying Margaret again and his mouth became a grin and his eyes glowed in secret fantasy and desire. He knelt down on the soil beside Margaret and, extending a pointed finger, prodded her dress tentatively. He drew his finger back like lightning, but she had not noticed. She was busy getting a leek to stand up straight. And her fallen hair prevented her from seeing anything at her side.

He poked again, feeling the soft flesh under her breast give to the pressure of his fingers, and his eyes widened in pleasure. He nudged his fingers against her again.

"Don't, Corky!" she said quietly, but Gavin had not heard. He moved his hand away, and instantly pressed his fingers through the falling folds of her gingham dress and deep into the soft of her waist. He felt her stiffen as she turned around.

"Don't, Corky...." she began, and he withdrew his hand and for a moment he felt and saw nothing as the thick red heat of his blush filled his face and neck.

But Margaret didn't scream and there was no fear on her face. Instead, she slowly smiled a knowing little smile and her eyes sparkled as she got to her feet and flicked the dirt from her dress.

Janey also got up, slightly puzzled because she had not seen anything that Gavin had done. "What's the matter, Maggie?" she asked.

"Do y' dee that to all the lasses?" Margaret asked Gavin, still smiling. Behind her, Janey stooped to pick up Corky's lead before he bolted again.

Gradually Gavin began to see the girl in front of him, and her question seeped through.

"Nah," he answered flatly, still very conscious of the blood roaring about his ears.

"Why d' y' do it to me, then?"

For a moment, Gavin prepared to reply, but the smiling girl gave him no opportunity.

"Would yer like to do it again?" she asked simply. "Well?" She stood openly in front of him, her arms close by her sides.

Janey began to grin when she saw the fear and desire in conflict on Gavin's face. But the desire was strong and his heart was beating fast. He began to grin. "Aye."

"Gan on then," invited Margaret.

Gavin's grin was more foolish-looking than ever. It was as if he was almost hiding behind it. He raised his arm slowly and pressed his outstretched and taut fingers against the girl's breast. She continued breathing normally and her face remained unchanged. Gavin ran his fingers down to her waist.

"You like it, don't you?"

He nodded excitedly. His blush and embarrassment were nearly gone.

"Would you like to kiss us, then?"

The hand was jerked back and the glow of pleasure in Gavin's eyes disappeared. For a split second he stood looking at her, and then he turned and ran from the allotment in big ungainly steps.

The girls began to laugh. Corky looked at them and began running round and round chasing his tail and tangling himself in the lead.

"Eh, what a funny lad! You're cruel, Maggie, having him on like that!"

"Ah'm not cruel. He's just a great thick lad in a garden. Ah don't think he hardly knows what a lass is." She became more reflective. "Ah wish I could get Len Hargreaves as easily as that."

Next day, Gavin did not go to the allotment and the girls did not go on their usual walk. Only a week later did he dare go back and although he waited until nearly half past six, the girls did not come. However, he soon forgot them because he discovered that he could easily poke and pinch girls in crowded places and not be caught out. He liked to stand outside the Edith Squire gate as the girls streamed past, and as they giggled at him he would grin back foolishly. Sometimes a lass would thump his arm and threaten to report him, but not often. Most of the girls rather liked it, and in any case he rarely hurt them or gave them any pain.

However, his reputation of being "one with the lasses" quickly grew, and the senior girls would say to the juniors when they saw him waiting at the gate, "There's Gavin Cooper. Ye'll have to watch him." And they would run past him, daring each other to speak to him.

Normally in school he would speak to no-one and during play-time he would stand stupidly as the boys whirled around him. But now it was different. They came up to him and taunted him.

"Who was it last night? Eh, Gavin?"

"Our Gavin's a lad with the girls, y' know!"

"Always chasing the lasses!"

For a moment he would enjoy the attention of the younger boys, but soon he would tire of their shouting. "Aw, get off! Gan away and play hide and seek!" And they would scatter before his flailing arms and re-form in a mocking ring. Then Gavin would run off to the changing rooms.

One day though, as he was slipping down to the Can to await the reassuring darkness, he bumped into Dennis and Barry and another boy called Colin. Usually Dennis would pass him by without saying anything, but after a wink at his pals he called to Gavin. "Where y' gannin', then?"

"Ah'm ganning to me Dad's allotment," said Gavin, obviously lying. He was actually walking in the opposite direction.

"Oh, aye. We're gannin' up into the fields for a walk. D' yer want to come?"

"There's gan to be girlies, Gavin!" said Barry, unable to hold back. "Lasses. Real lasses!"

"Are y' coming then?" repeated Dennis.

"Where?"

"Up in the fields, man," Barry chuckled again.

"Aye," Gavin had decided suddenly. "Ah'll come."

So he tagged along with them as they walked through the remaining streets of the estate and the other boys asked him about his latest activities with the Edith Squire girls.

"When you're getting married, then?" asked Barry with mock seriousness. When Gavin looked puzzled, Barry nearly collapsed with laughter.

"Do yer knar Janey Sutherland?" asked Dennis.

"Nah."

"Well, she says she knars ye. And Margaret Mahon."

At the corner, by a block of large grey concrete council-flats, they met June.

Dennis called to her. "Where's Thelma, then?"

"She said she couldn't come. Her Mam's in hospital and she says her Dad's making her visit."

"Are ye still coming, then?"

"Aye. But she might come later, she said."

They set off on the path to the fields, Dennis, Barry and June in front, and Colin and Gavin walking behind.

June had not changed much. Her hair was a little longer and now almost met under her chin, and her eyes and gently rounded nose were the same. Over her face there was a little makeup: lipstick to remove a hardness from the outline of her lips and light powder on her cheeks, stopping abruptly below her chin and contrasting with the whiteness of her neck. Over her tight skirt and frilled white blouse she wore a warm coat of blue cloth, but there were no nylons to relieve the redness of her calves or her sore heels as they slipped in and out of white patent leather stilettos.

Soon after reaching the silence that was in the fields, they came in sight of an old barn. Once, it had belonged to Mr Barker but now it was disused. The wet autumn had already caused some of the boards of its wooden walls to fall away.

When they got near the entrance, Dennis went inside, beckoning the others to stay back. In a moment his head reappeared. "Alright, there's no one in."

One by one, they all bent low into the half-light within. Gavin was the last to enter. Inside, the ground was covered in a light carpet of dirtied straw. Light filtered through cracks in the walls and roof, and over in a corner there were some newspapers, a few old tins and a battered and dirty old paraffin stove.

"Must've been a tramp," Barry remarked.

Colin nodded in agreement.

At one end of the barn there was a small loft, like a minstrel's gallery, and beneath it a pile of old straw. Leading up to the loft there was a simple ladder made of rough pine logs.

"Alright, girlie!" Dennis grabbed June round the waist and swung her round so that the smell of her powder was close by his face.

"Alright, then?" he repeated a little more softly.

"Aye," she smiled back at him.

"Then give us a kiss, then."

She leaned forward and pecked his cheek.

"Hey, that's no good," joked Dennis.

"Aw, Dennis," mocked Barry. "Ye divvn't knar what ter dee."

"He's better than ye anyhow!" returned June in a hard voice from behind Dennis's protecting arm.

"Gan on then, Dennis. Hurry up," said Barry. He was becoming a little agitated.

So Dennis led June over to the ladder and she mounted the rough pine steps and he followed her. Gavin watched them from the darkness, and he was surprised and excited. He could smell the cheap perfume June was wearing. Up in the loft he saw June take off her coat and spread it on the hay. Then she sat down and lay back, pressing down on the crackling straw. Dennis got down beside her and Gavin could see no more.

Colin and Barry took less interest and went over to examine the paraffin stove. "Any paraffin in?"

Barry shook it. "Aye."

"Can you make it work?"

"P'rhaps," replied Barry. He turned to Gavin. "Can ye?"

"Me?" said Gavin.

"Aye."

"Nah."

"Just a dumb kiddie, you. Aren't y', kidder?"

"Aye."

Colin looked at Barry and grinned. Then Gavin grinned.

Above them, the straw rustled and out of the dusty darkness came whisperings, sighs and little moans and grunts of pain and pleasure. There were long times of silence with only a little rustling in the straw. Then they could hear Dennis's voice but not his words, and once June gave a little squeal and cried out, "Aw Dennis, divvn't dee that!"

For what seemed like a long time, the boys stood silent and listening and then Dennis got up and was coming down the ladder. They started forward.

"You want anyone else?" called Dennis up to the loft.

"Aye, if you like," came back the answer, thickly and slow.

Barry ran up the steps.

Nearly twenty minutes later, when Colin came down, running his hands through his hair to straighten it, Dennis called again.

"You want Gavin, then?"

"May as well."

They all turned to Gavin, and Colin began to grin again. Gavin had paused by the ladder.

"Well, gan up!" said Dennis. "She won't eat yer."

Gavin climbed up the steps evenly, but not quickly. In front of him, stretched out on her coat and leaning on one elbow, was June. Her hair was a little untidy and she had kicked off her shoes, but her blouse and skirt were not disarranged. She shook her hair as she had done on the steam-roller, and it fell into place either side of her face. Her eyes were soft and she beckoned and held out a hand. "Come on, then."

He knelt down beside her with his eyes fixed on hers, and the grin returned to his face. For a moment they watched each other, motionless, and then she nodded her head and smiled and he moved his hand over to her breast and pressed it none too gently. She squealed and caught him and pulled him down with her. Before he could react, her arms were around his body and she was clinging to him and almost crushing him. Now she steadied his head and pressed her lips to his, but his lips were soft and wide and like jelly. They had no form or purpose and only fumbled about the edge of her mouth. She pressed her tongue against his tightly-clenched teeth, but there was no response. His body had become stiffened and his arms were straight by his sides. He shuddered a little as his mouth opened, and he began turning his head from side to side, aimlessly rubbing his lips against her cheek. For an instant there was fear in her eyes; she half tensed, kicking her leg out and catching him in the soft of the groin. He cried into her cheek, but then suddenly relaxed, wound his arms round her and pulled her to him. But in a moment she had slipped away and rolled over so that she came to be on top of him. For a while he struggled a little and then his movements gradually ceased and they lay, tight, cheek against cheek for some minutes.

Now she eased over to one side and began gently running her hands down his shirt and over the hot hardening inbetween his legs, so that he felt the soft warmth seeping into his body wherever they were close.

For a while they just lay there, still in the straw, and he could feel his heart beating behind his eyes.

Then she turned and began kissing him again, but now he had lost all control of his lips. They drooled wide against her powdered cheek and he was panting and his heart beat in his temples. Her kissing became more insistent and he could feel the rhythmic rubbing of her hand against the stiffness in his trousers. In moments, a terrible tension seemed to rise in his body, overwhelming even his panting breath, and suddenly his groin was throbbing and in his confused pleasure and release he pushed her away with a little cry. In the same moment, a flash of pain penetrated his warmth. And again. And a voice.

"What're you deeing with our June? Eh?"

Again there was stabbing pain in his side and he recognised Dennis.

"What are y' doing, eh?" Dennis carefully punctuated his last word with a powerful jab of his pointed shoe into Gavin's ribs.

Another voice began to shout as Gavin rolled away from June and gasped and cried out. Standing over him were the lads. He could not see their faces properly, only menacing grey shapes and the flash of their eyes.

"What you deeing to her, eh?!"

Gavin cowered back and gasped again. As the shoe jabbed and other shoes followed, he screamed.

"We seen what you been deeing!"

"Good with the lasses, eh?!"

"Do you want any more?!"

"Keep off our June! D' y' hear?"

"D' y' want any more?"

The voices were ringing in his ears, harsh and cruel with the kicking and jabbing, and they were laughing and he couldn't even properly see their faces.

"No! No! No!" He screamed. "No! No more!"

"Lassies, we mean," shrieked Barry in a hysterical laugh as he jabbed his shoe again.

"No! No more! Please! Gerroff! No!"

They all roared in hideous laughter and even June joined in, and her teeth seemed to sparkle. Gavin was shuddering with fear. His legs twitched backwards and forwards.

"Well, gan home then! What're y' waiting for?"

"Aw, look at his legs!"

And as they all began laughing again, Gavin squirmed away from them, got up to the ladder, but half fell down the pine steps. At the bottom he began to cry out again but there was not time to stop. The screams and laughs were close behind him, threatening to get him, to do him, to kill him and so he scrambled to his feet and ran from the building, out into the cooling of the evening.

At first there was no pain, only fear and a deep and curious numbness. He ran blindly across the fields, past the darkening hedgerows and deep ditches until he was safely in the lights of the estate again. There were no shouts and thudding steps behind him and so he slowed down. He was washed with perspiration and his heart was thumping all over his body and his side was beginning a dull ache.

After a few minutes, he had pains every time he breathed in. The bruising on his ribs would come up dark and blue. Tears began to seep from his eyes and the pains made it worse. He slipped away to the pipe in the playground and sat in it, whimpering softly. For what seemed like a long time he just sat there, panting and catching his breath. Gradually though, he settled, and the pain softened a little, and then he became aware of a cold stickiness in his pants, but it was only as he wiped his arm across his tear-stained face that he smelled her perfume and remembered the warmth of her body.

# FOURTEEN

Thelma was quite different from June. She was a little taller but much more heavily built. It would not be fair to call her fat, but she was liberally insulated against the cold and any stray slaps from the lads. She had tinted her hair a ginger blonde, and whereas June's was long and smooth, hers was brushed back off her face in a wiry whirl. She always wore heavy make-up. Her grey-green eyes were lost behind iridescent blue eye-shadow, and her thin blonde eyebrows were drawn out with dark eyebrow pencil. Thelma had a wide neck, just a hint of a double chin, thick lips straight from a cartoonist's sketch board, and she liked chewing gum and showing her large white teeth. She was standing by a pillar and her face was in shadow because the sun was quite high and it was Saturday afternoon.

Dennis and June and the rest of the gang were also in shadow but standing further back beneath the concrete canopy. There was no wind, and for an April day it was quite warm, talking out in the open sunlight.

The sun was not so high and hot as it would be in a few weeks' time, but it was dazzling and very warm for the time of year. The sky was clear blue and there were a few wisps of clouds in lines running diagonally across the azure vault over the street. A bus roared past, cutting off the sun from the hot white concrete of the flats above the pillared canopy, and was followed by an eddying cloud of dust as it rounded the corner.

The Can was open but none of the lads had been in. Inside were a couple of workmen having late pie and chips, and instead of the juke-box, an LP of a popular American musical was playing softly. The lads would not start to go in until about five o' clock, when the others had returned from the football match in the city. Then the light would begin to fade, and soon the juke-box would begin and the neon sign of the Billy Can would light up and twinkle.

But now all was quiet. Dennis sat on his bike, long brown hair flapping over his forehead. He tossed it back over his head. "D' y' see Johnny Lamb and the Cutlets? Number five now."

"Aye, Ah knar," said Thelma, lolling against the pillar and chewing.

"They're not. They're seven," said Barry.

"They are. They're five. It's on the chart in Walkers. Ah was in there this morning, getting me LP." Thelma began to grin as she chewed.

"See, Barry, ye're wrong."

"What's yer LP, then?" asked Barry.

"Jacob Matthews in Paris."

"What's he sing, then?"

Between chews, Thelma rattled the titles off: " 'Won't You', 'Too Young', 'Arabian Shake', 'Too Much Time on my Hands', 'Arthur Brown', 'Jacob's Clearway,' 'When,' 'Scootah Hootah'…. You know the one." She began to sing softly to herself and her dress swung from side to side.

> " 'Hootah Scootah, Scootah Hootah.
> When you're up beside me baby
> With your arms around me baby
> Then I know we'll go
> Not too fast and not too slow
> On my

Hootah Scootah, Scootah Hootah.

Today and every day....'

Aw, man. It's smashin'."

"Ah like 'Jacob's Clearway'," said June.

"Who does the backing, then?" asked Barry.

"The Laddermen, of course," said Thelma and June, aghast. "Y' know, they used to be the Slavedrivers, then Jacob heard them and now they always back him."

"Oh," said Barry. He was eager to change the conversation. "Hey! Look who's coming!" He pointed to the figure coming up through the alternating light and dark spaces under the pillars. Thelma moved further into the shadow to get a better view.

"Who is it?" she asked.

"It's that stupid Gavin Cooper," said Barry. "He come with us to the barn. Yer knar, in the fields. The other neet. Stupid little bugger, him." Barry cupped his hands to shout at Gavin.

"Nah! Divvn't man!" said Dennis. "Let's see what he's gan to say."

"Does he gan round with yer, then?" asked Thelma.

"Nah. But the stupid little bugger canna take a hint."

Gavin was walking up to them without any hesitation. There was no reason to lurk in the shadows now. It was the first time he had seen Dennis since he had run from the barn. They had kept out of his way, but now he had found them. He began grinning as he made out their faces more clearly, and his pace quickened a little. But June did not smile at him. Her eyes still sparkled, but behind her lipstick her lips were a hard mocking line. When he came right up to the group he glanced at Thelma, then at Dennis.

"Well, kidder. What do ye's want?"

"Nowt," answered Gavin. The grin had left his face.

Dennis' and Barry's eyes bored into him. "Well, what yer hangin' round for?!"

"Ah'm not."

"Why y' come over here, then?" said Barry, menacing Gavin with his fist. "The Can's for us. We divvn't want yer round here, see!"

Thelma watched, chewing slowly. Her grey eyes had seen it all before and she was quickly becoming bored.

But Gavin did not fall back at Barry's menacing. He looked beyond to Dennis and June.

Dennis was becoming paler and his face was set and solid. "We don't want you, Gavin Cooper, see?" he said slowly between clenched teeth.

June's face was smiling and her eyes flashed, but it was a cruel smile, one of contempt, cold and empty.

Gavin's eyes flicked from Dennis and caught June's smile.

Dennis started forward, white-faced. "Get out, son," he hissed. "Get out before Ah have to...."

Barry began to nudge and buffet Gavin away. "Come on, move! Move! Or we'll kill yer! Move! Move!"

Now Gavin was against the rough concrete pillar.

"Move! Move, lad!"

But he couldn't. Barry hemmed him in against the stone.

"Ah can't. Ye won't let us past."

"Gan on, pass!" Barry spoke with a mocking assurance.

Gavin squirmed aside, but Barry's arm was there. He tried the other side, but Barry's arm was there too.

"Let us past, man!" Tears were beginning to fill Gavin's eyes.

"Gan on, then! Baby!" Barry let him past and thumped him hard in the kidneys.

Gavin gasped with the pain and stumbled in the road. He turned to them and his eyes flashed in anger. "Barry Burton! Ah'll kill ye! Ah'll kill ye!"

"Come on, then."

Thelma stopped chewing and her thick lips spread into a wide grin when Gavin did not come forward and instead limped across the road, holding the dull pain in his side.

He saw June only a few times after that. The short Easter holiday had gone and the summer term began at William Squire. Once or twice he saw June coming out of school, but Dennis, who was a school prefect now and so left school a little earlier, was always waiting for her and they would hold hands and go off walking to the bus-stop together. Gavin would turn off in the other direction because he never went near Dennis or the others if he could help it.

Instead he enjoyed the attention of the more foolish boys from the first and second years. They would stand around him in the playground at break because they were eager to talk to a senior boy. The more astute of the younger boys had nothing to do with him. They knew Dennis and some of the big lads in the senior forms. They knew that Dennis despised Gavin and they liked to mirror his feelings to please and impress him. But there were always a few who would listen to Gavin's wild fantasies.

They heard about his girlfriend June, about how he went walks with her every weekend, about how he was in a gang and how they went raiding and pinching stuff. Some of them laughed at him because they knew part of the truth, but the others listened and watched him, wide-eyed. They only half-believed him, but this was what they wanted to be like when they were in the senior forms.

Gavin said less than ever to boys in his own form. The art-master noticed that he was quieter than usual. But his work in paints was wilder and more colourful than ever. He would sit by himself in a corner, mumbling and humming to himself and covering the paper with thick coloured strokes from his brush.

"What is it? What is that, boy?" the art-master asked.

Gavin did not look up but continued applying a brilliant yellow-orange.

"It's for me girlfriend and me," he replied, in a faraway and absorbed voice.

"Oh, I see," said the art-master, staring at it with his head on one side and a twinkle in his eye. "I see."

A few days later, Gavin's geography-master found a JOONE=GAVIN on the back page of his book.

"What's this scrawl? What have I said about scrawling in books?" he boomed over Gavin's shoulder. "Don't do it, Cooper.

Don't do it, lad!"

But Gavin took no notice. He carved JOONE, a heart and arrow and his own name on the underside of his desk lid, and scrawled JOONE over one of the toilet walls in the new toilet block.

Mr Barclay soon found out. Gavin admitted it openly, making no attempt at deceit. Somehow this openness seemed to make Mr Barclay even more annoyed and exasperated. "Why did you do it? Why do you go scrawling on the good clean walls, man?"

"Ah don't know, sir."

"Well, you'll scrub everything that appears on any of the toilet walls for the next fortnight. You personally! Understand?"

"Yes, sir."

"Well, get a brush and soap and go and clean it up. You know where they are."

And when the other lads heard who was on wall-duty, all sorts of obscene pictures and messages appeared and Gavin tried to scrub them off before Mr Barclay could find them. But he wasn't quick enough, and Mr Barclay saw many of them and wondered whether he oughtn't to have beaten the lad after all.

At home, Gavin became more than ever bound up in himself. He began to say less and less to his mother and father, and instead of speaking to them he would sit at meals with an odd grin on his face.

Mr Cooper got really mad about him. "What are you looking so happy about?"

Gavin looked up from his plate and stared between his father and mother.

"Oh, he's like that all day long. Just sits up in his bedroom humming to himself." Mrs Cooper was fed up with him.

Then Gavin spoke slowly, sounding out each vowel and consonant like a child learning to speak properly. "Ah've got a girl-friend called June." Then his eyes re-focussed on his parents and the grin was as broad as ever.

"Not that again!" said his father. "How can you have a girl-friend? You never get out anywhere!"

And he didn't. Now the weeks were passing and summer was

creeping in. Light in the evenings became light at night and the lights of the Can were switched on later and later. But Gavin never went down to the Can. Gone were the days when he would stare in at the world from the shadows. The shadows in the real world had gone. Now Gavin had to make his own. Then he could feel safe.

He never went to the fields any more, now that Dennis and the other lads were often there, but then he didn't need to. Instead he spent more and more of his time in his bedroom, humming and singing quietly to himself, and always some coloured crayons before him. He used these to decorate the margins of comics and some of his books. Many of his books which already had blue on them were now covered in red and yellow. These were the colours he used most, and when a book became saturated with new colours, he wrote "FOR JOONE" on the first page, each letter in a different colour.

One day he became angry with some of his books and, grabbing the nearest comic, he began to tear it to pieces. The pieces became smaller and smaller until they were little fingernails of paper, print and colour. Then he laid each tiny scrap on the floor and began to arrange them in a huge mosaic. Those scraps with no strong colouring on them were quickly covered in red or blue. When he had finished he stood up and admired the hundreds of gaily coloured scraps. He opened the door and went out on to the landing. "Mam! Look what Ah've made!"

But there was no answer. Mrs Cooper was away over on the other side of the town again, and when Gavin returned to his bedroom, the draught disarranged the patterns which had come from his mind and given him such satisfaction.

"Where are you?" he whispered as he knelt down to replace the pieces. "Where are you? Where are you? You've gone. You're gone. You're gone." He repeated this over and over to himself in a flat voice.

Then he found that the other books and colours were still there and safe, and he took one of them and held it in front of him and laughed with his dry high-pitched laugh.

Sundays were an important day because it was then that he would go down to the allotment and tend his leek plants. Mr Cooper was glad Gavin still liked the allotment. It was the only pleasure in his life and he was pleased to see his son's interest growing. Gavin usually went on Sunday because his father was not there. He could be by himself, alone with his little patch of ground. In it he transplanted some tiny lettuces, radishes and cabbage plants, and watered them every time the ground was dry.

The damaged leek seemed to pick up, too. At first after he had watered it, it became very limp and sickly, but during the week Mr Cooper gave it some of his secret leek food and as a result it did not die. Gavin was pleased that the leek was not dying any more, and pleased that the rest of his garden was growing.

One Sunday, Mr Cooper came down to watch him gardening. At last he had decided to let Gavin have the secret of his recipe. He sat down on the old seat whilst Gavin continued hoeing lightly round the cabbages.

"What'll you do with those plants when they are ready?" Mr Cooper wanted to test his son's knowledge.

"Dig them up," replied Gavin.

"Uh huh," murmured Mr Cooper, lighting a cigarette. He inhaled deeply. "Aye. And what are you going to do then?"

Gavin looked up. "Give some to me Mam, but keep most for June. We'll need them one day."

"And who's June?"

"Me girlfriend," answered Gavin sullenly.

"By, Gavin, you're a funny lad." And Mr Cooper went away without giving Gavin his secret.

Towards the end of the summer term, the Youth Employment Officer came to William Squire. He always came at the end of the Easter and summer terms and interviewed all the lads who were fifteen and due to leave school. He gave them a card and tried to fix them up with an employer for a job, but often he had a difficult problem getting some of the boys accepted by any employer. Those boys were dull and slow or quick-minded and indolent, and others were just not capable of understanding what the responsibility of earning really meant. With all the boys in the lower streams, finding jobs which they could hold and keep was a subject which particularly interested Mr Manners. He spent a great deal of his time keeping in contact with the factories on the trading estate and arranging trips for the senior boys, and when the Youth Employment Officer came for the interviews he was at his busiest.

After the main run of interviews was over, Mr Manners gave Mr Bertram, the Y.E.O., a list of eight boys who would not be fifteen until early in the first term of the next school year. Mr Manners felt that these boys needed special attention as far as getting jobs, and Gavin was fifth on the list.

Mr Bertram was a smallish man with swarthy skin, wavy oiled black hair and piercing dark eyes. He had little black hairs creeping onto the backs of his hands, and his fingers were slim and strong. He took the list in his hand and slipped his glasses back on. Then he smiled. "I see, Wilf. These are the real problem cases."

"Yes, I suppose so. Anyhow, I'd be pleased if you would have a word with them. Jeffries there, he might make carpentry, and Johnson…."

At quarter past three the next day, Gavin stood outside the library door and knocked lightly. As there was no reply, he knocked again.

"Come in," said a cheerful voice.

Gavin pushed open the door and saw Mr Bertram sitting in the sun at a table by the windows. On the left of his papers and notes, a green fern plant clambered round split canes in a large, dull-glazed pot.

"Come in, son, and sit down."

Gavin glanced around the empty library, at the island shelves and their shining polythene-covered books. Then he sat in the wooden chair opposite Mr Bertram.

"Well, now, let's see." Mr Bertram ran his finger over some papers. "You're … Cooper. Ah, yes. Gavin Cooper."

Gavin's face remained still.

"Gavin Cooper?" repeated Mr Bertram, raising one eyebrow.

"Yes, sir," answered Gavin in an expressionless voice.

Mr Bertram seemed for a moment to be lost in thought. "Ah yes, well then ... er ... Cooper, let's see what we can do for you. You know that I am here to help you get a job for when you leave school?"

"Yes, sir."

"Well, it's important that you don't have just any job, but that the one that you have will be really useful for you, one which you will enjoy and one which you will be good at."

"Yes, sir."

Mr Bertram picked up his mottled green fountain pen and pulled out a clean white card. "Now, have you thought of anything?"

Gavin answered without hesitation: "No, sir." Then his eyes flicked to the pen.

"I see. Well, your full name is Gavin Cooper?"

"Yes."

"Birthday, 23rd September 1950. Address, 32 Bolton Street." He paused. "That makes you fourteen and three-quarters now. You'll be fifteen next term." He blotted the card. "Now, what about jobs? What are you interested in?"

"I don't know, sir."

"What does your Dad do?" Mr Bertram stared at the typed words "Factory night guard" on one of his papers.

"He's a watchie."

"Oh, I see. A night-watchman. At a factory?"

"Yes."

"What would he like you to do when you leave school?"

"Ah think he wants us to be an electrician at the works."

"Do you want to be an electrician?"

"No, sir."

"You don't feel you could really make a go of it?"

"No."

Mr Bertram glanced again at Gavin's report summary. "Well,

you're probably wise. You must do something which you feel you can do satisfactorily. What about your outside interests?"

Gavin had been examining his worn-out and grubby fingernails as they rested on his lap. He looked up at the Y.E.O.

"I mean, what do you do when you are not in school?"

"Ah gan out in the fields."

"To play football?"

"Nah. Just cos Ah like bein' out in the fields."

"And do you go with your friends?" Mr Bertram was studying Gavin's face with a new interest.

"Nah."

"So you go by yourself."

"Aye."

They stared at each other for a few seconds, and then Gavin's face lit up with a new energy. "Sometimes Ah gan out with me girlfriend. She's called June."

"Oh, I see. And you meet her friends?"

Gavin spoke more hurriedly now. "Aye, and sometimes we gan to the fields."

"I see," said Mr Bertram thoughtfully. "So you like the open air...."

"An' we go away together to our own house, an' we have all this country, an' fields, an' servants-"

"Yes, well, this doesn't really help me find you a job." Mr Bertram had cut in sharply, but now he spoke gently: "Does it?"

Gavin became dulled again. "No, sir."

"Well, what do you do in the open air, then? Do you fancy the Forestry Commission? Plenty of outdoor life there. Or what about gardening? Working in parks and so on. Laying out gardens."

Gavin began to speak hurriedly again. "Me Dad has an allotment, and Ah dig in there. Ah've got me own vegetables and a big leek what me Dad give us. It was dying like, but now it's coming back. Ah watered it and it's coming back."

"So you would like gardening?"

"Aye. And in autumn Ah'll show me leek and win big prizes and then we'll gan away in the country again."

Mr Bertram began to fill the card in with his fountain pen. "You obviously are keen on gardening. So we'll see what we can do." He blotted the card again. "Alright, Cooper."

Gavin was still far away.

"Alright?" repeated Mr Bertram.

"Yes, sir."

"Alright. You can go back to your lesson now."

Gavin got up and without nodding or shaking Mr Bertram's outstretched hand, he walked over to the door. Mr Bertram watched him closely. "Tell me, Cooper...."

Gavin turned round in the doorway. "Yes, sir."

"What do you like doing in the fields?"

"Sitting up in trees, sir."

Mr Bertram's face did not flicker. "I see. Thank you. Goodbye."

Gavin shut the door, and Mr Bertram sat down with his papers. "Well, well," he laughed lightly to himself. "Wilf's got a right one there." Later that afternoon he was to speak to Mr Manners about the interview.

Mr Ramsey was out of the classroom when Gavin returned. The class had heard footsteps in the corridor and immediately the buzz of conversation disappeared, but when Gavin appeared through the door he was greeted by a series of guffaws and calls.

"Eh, Gavvers!" "Eh, Cooper!"

"Been to see the big man, eh?" grinned a huge fellow with long greased hair called Davis. "What's he say to y', Cooper? Eh?"

Gavin walked up to his desk and sat down. The boys at either side turned round to him.

"Have yer got a card?"

"Nah," said Gavin sullenly.

"Yer gan ter get a job then?"

"Aye."

A little dirty boy with slanting eyes and red hair stood up in his desk and leered across at Davis. "Y' knar what he's gan ter be, then? He'll be a bingo caller!"

"Why no. He canna even count, man!"

"What you gan to be, then?" asked Davis, turning to grin at Gavin.

"Ah divvn't knar."

"He doesn't knar."

"Whey, neither dee I! Neither dee ye," grinned the boy with the red hair.

"Well, ye knar, ye're just thick, Tommy!" said Davis.

"Like ye."

"Shurrup or Ah'll kill yer."

"What'll June say when yer don't even know? Eh?" asked Tommy.

"Ah'll tell her."

"June.... That's Cooper's lass, isn't it?" cried Davis. Two of the boys began to laugh. "Tell us, man! Tell us!" shouted Davis. Two of the boys went over to him and whispered in his ear. He stood up straight again, laughing. "You heard about June? Eh, Cooper?"

Gavin was alive again. "Na! What about June? Ye don't know her."

The lads that knew began to giggle again.

"She's a fortnight overdue," one of the lads blurted out.

The rest quickly caught on and began jeering at Gavin. "Eh, Cooper!" "Eh, Gavvers!" "Been on the nest?! Eh, lad!" And all the voices rose to a high pitch again.

"June'll kill y' when she sees y'!"

"Ye'll have to pay every week!"

A little stupid boy on the back row began to spin round and round in the aisle between the desks. "June Simpson's gan ter have a baby! Gan ter have a baby! Gan ter have a baby!"

Mr Ramsey appeared in the doorway and stood listening to the din for a few seconds. Then he shouted above them all: "Quiet! Stop that racket at once!"

Almost immediately the noise became a buzz, then a silence, and the class slunk off back to their desks like cowardly dogs.

At the end of the afternoon, June came out of school with a cluster of girls around her. She was smiling and laughing with them, and carrying her leather school bag before her as she always did. When Gavin saw the sparkle in her eyes and the happiness in her face, the chattering giggling girls about her and the group of William Squire boys going up to meet her, he ducked behind a low wall by the bus shelter and began running away from the houses and towards the open country.

Dennis was in the knot of senior William Squire boys. At first he wasn't sure, but as June and the girls came towards him, he knew that it had begun at last, and his whole body was overcome with relief.

# FIFTEEN

Gavin ran straight up the road and away from the school until the school buildings and playground were drawn out of his field of vision. He did not look round. Below him, at the bus stop, the noise of their chattering and screaming and laughing continued. He could still hear them, all clustered around her and laughing, and although the sound was behind him it pressed him on to run faster and harder. His head was jerking from side to side and his arms were flailing and swinging out of phase with his big, clumsy strides. He continued running all the way up the uneven grass verge. Each step made the school smaller, and the cries at the bus stop became fainter.

Near the summit of the hill, he tripped in a drainage runnel and almost fell flat on his face. He picked himself up and paused for a moment, and listened. There was nothing. At last all the sounds were gone, lost in the pounding of his heart and the sharp panting of his breath.

A green bus appeared at the top of the hill. Gavin looked up and saw it begin its acceleration for the downward run. As it was almost on top of him he darted across in front of the huge silver radiator. The car that was overtaking the bus did not see him until the last moment. Gavin was filled with the screeching tyres of the crash stop, there was spinning, streaking earth, and then he had broken through the hedge and was running and stumbling down the side of a field of green wheat.

He vaguely heard the bus-driver shouting, more voices, and then the bus revving again as it set off down the hill.

At the end of the field he came to a wide but shallow ditch. Without pausing, he leaped over and fell head-long, hands out-stretched against the bars of a low piece of fencing. As he waited, his face pale with fear, he heard again the thudding of his heart and felt throbbing all over his body. Now he was breathing more slowly but the throbbing seemed to be shaking his limbs. He waited and strained for any sound beyond his body.

But there was no one on the path behind him. He turned his head and at the same time he heard the bus pull away from the stop by the school. He could see that it had left no one behind. They had all been sucked in, wiped from the pavement, and were now being carried away. He smiled.

Slowly he got to his feet and looked back at the whole frontage of the school buildings. Suddenly it had all become very silent and peaceful, as if the school had gone to sleep.

He nodded and spoke aloud. "That's how yer all ought ter be."

Then he looked round at the field on the other side of the fence. It was all deep grass, sharp, shining and crisp. Dotted here and there were buttercups, wild parsley and ox-eye daisies. He climbed up the fence and as he swung his leg over he felt the new soft bruise where the car had so finely glanced him. The twinge made him cramp and call out in pain. Another small movement made him kick his leg out in reflex and, losing his balance, he fell into the long grass.

Almost immediately, he was on his feet again and jogging along, moaning a little under his breath. He began talking to himself, flatly and rhythmically. "This is my country … this is my country … Ah'm all right … they're going to kill us … no, no, no … they're going to … this is my country … Ah want to…."

Behind him was a narrow trail of flattened grass. There were beads of moisture on the stems and insects rose all around.

The hill began to slope gently downwards. Running was made easier, but Gavin did not quicken or lengthen his step. He just jogged on, letting his head hang loosely so that it jerked up and down with the sharp rhythm. Words were shaken from him like seeds from a poppy head. "They don't know ... no, no, no ... don't know ... they might kill all of them ... they're going to kill us ... no know ... nobody knows ... nobody.... Ah must tell them ... they would just kill them and trample them.... Ah want to ... Ah must find the house ... tell them what to do ... they don't know ... don't ... no, no...."

On the far side of the sunlit field was a small copse of pine trees. The trail of flattened grass led right up to the fencing that surrounded the copse. Gavin looked up at the dark green branches that swayed above his head. His eyes grew wide as he stared upwards. Further and further up they went, following the straight black trunks.

Inside the copse, the trunks were stark and bare, bristling with dead brush. They were like pillars upholding the green roof above. Between the crowded trunks, Gavin could see pale white light filtering through from the far side of the wood. A gentle breeze breathed over the field, and the pines swayed backwards and forwards in a slow and measured motion.

Gavin found a hole in the fence and crawled through. He continued talking to himself, almost whispering. "They be in here ... in here ... don't want them to kill me ... must tell them ... they'll know what to do ... they'll be in here ... servants... they can pick them ... mustn't trample ... must tell them."

Now he was on his feet and moving into the darkness under the trees. The air was moist and cool and the odour of pine needles and damp wood was all around him. He stared up at the tree-tops and then quickly to either side. When he was satisfied, he leaned forward and spoke in a harsh whisper. "June! June! Ah've got a job, now! Now Ah'll be able to grow all we need!" He glanced aside again. "That'll help pay...." He listened. Above, the pines rustled

and swayed soothingly. The light flickered in patches on the brown
pine needles. He looked upwards and then shouted blindly. "June!
That'll help pay, won't it?! June! Come on!" He ran forwards, was
enclosed by another group of trees and cried out again. "June!
Come on! Wait for the servants! Wait for them! June!"

But there was no reply. The majestic trees bent softly and bowed
in the breeze, serenely as ever.

Gavin ran forward again. At the same time, a stronger wind blew
through the wood and all the trees bent together. But they made no
noise. Then the wind died away and far above Gavin heard crows
calling to one another. Only a few feet in front of him there was a
patch of moist green grass lit in a dancing but constant light.

He sat down on the grass and cupped his hands to his mouth.
"June! You coming?!" Then very quietly, he said to himself, "Ah'll
wait for yer. Ah'll wait. We can go and look for camps … or
anything."

He did not look around again. Instead, he lowered his head down
in between his knees and began idly pulling out little tufts of moist
grass. Gradually he piled up a tiny green haystack, but the wind
grew again, the trees bent, and the stack was pushed to one side and
disarranged. For some minutes he sat in the flickering patch of
light, silent. Then he lifted his head and shouted. "Ah'll go and get
them if y' like! Ah want to! June! Come into the fields! June!"

He listened again, but there was nothing. He made a little
groaning sound, rolled forward and began to crawl away from the
grass and over the fine dust and pine needles. All the time he kept
lifting up his head and calling. "Come into the fields, June! That's
what we want! They'll be waiting at the house! At the big house!"

Every few yards he stopped and listened. But it was always the
same. The silence drove him further. He called more desperately.
"June! June! Don't trample on it! Remember they're coming." He
began rolling over, kicking out and protecting himself. "No! No!
Please, geroff! No more! No! June! No…. Come on, man!" He
reached out and pulled himself up onto a fallen log, his jeans and
jersey covered in pine needles. In front, he could see the blinding

light at the edge of the wood.

Soon he was speaking to himself very quietly, so that no one could have possibly heard him. "Come on, man.... Ah didn't mean to trample on them ... them servants should know...." He buried his face on his sleeve. "Ah'll tell you what ... Ah'll wait ... Ah'll wait, and when Ah look up y'll be there." The wind blew and the trees nodded in agreement.

After a minute he lifted up his eyes and stared into the light. A little shiver shook through his body. "Come on ... no ... noooo...!" Tears filled his eyes. He was whispering. "No ... remember ... Ah didn't trample ... Ah didn't ... no, no, nooo...." Gradually his words faded and dissolved into quiet whining sobs.

Then behind him something was pushing through the brush. There were twigs crackling. A voice. "Hey! Who's there?! Are you alright?!"

Gavin jerked up with a little gasp. His eyes were wild and when he looked round, he saw two figures coming through the pines, silhouetted against the light beyond. They were bent low and running.

In a flash, he was crashing toward the light in terror, shrieking and screaming. "They've come to trample...! Ah didn't mean...! No! No!"

When he reached the wire fence on the other side, he half jumped, half tripped over. He landed, legs flying, a screaming bundle. Instantly, he disentangled and began running blindly, desperately, faster than he had ever done in his whole life. The grass and brambles were a blur at his feet. The horizon suddenly lifted and he was flat again. For a moment his breath was hot against the grass and his legs and arms were thrashing backwards and forwards like a young animal pinned. He rolled over and began crawling. Then brambles tore and cut his hands. Unsteadily he got to his feet and continued running and stumbling down the hill.

There was no path down the rough hillside until he came to an area of thick gorse bushes. Here, there was a narrow twisting track and soon he was hidden from sight. Being hidden made no difference. He went plunging blindly on, fending off the worst branches with outstretched hands.

Far above him, the sun lit the swaying pines at the edge of the copse and for a moment two workmen in overalls appeared at the fence. Then they moved back into the trees again.

The hill led down to a broad, flat valley. Laid across the valley were some of the factories of the trading estate and beyond them, rows of back-to-back houses crawled over the hillside towards the city. On the other side of the gorse, the hill became steeper but Gavin did not slacken his pace. He seemed to welcome the added speed. He had lost all control of his running but his face was glowing and he seemed to be shouting and laughing at the top of his voice. When he came to the edge of a cliff of soil, the turf crackled and gave way, and he slipped and slithered to the bottom. His feet touched grass again and suddenly he was still. All around him little balls of soil rolled on. Slowly he sat up and began to examine the ground in front of him.

He was almost on the flat plain of the valley. Nearby, some young birch trees clutched at the hillside, their silver-grey bark reflecting the bright sunshine. Spread over the land in front of him were the remains of a bombed-out factory, a local reminder of raids in the war. The first and second floors had completely disappeared. All that remained were low crumbling walls of a pale brick, piles of rubbish and debris and some empty but upright door frames. The whole area was softened and almost completely covered by field grass. In between the walls, huge stinging-nettles grew, wild, fierce and free.

There was a little smile on Gavin's face and he spoke softly. "My country ... my country ... my house ... mustn't trample on the big house ... my house ... mustn't trample...." He glanced up behind him but there was only the broken turf and grass of the overhang. The wood had gone.

As soon as he was on his feet, he began to clamber down into the ruined building. "My house ... my house ... send them all ... no, no.... Ah'll pick them ... all," he kept repeating to himself.

In this part, the nettles had not grown so profusely. He was able to edge along a white brick wall. As he pushed aside the trailing grass, he dislodged little particles of dried mortar and soil. The nettles swayed in the breeze and some of them stroked the back of his hand. The prickling pain made him smile, then laugh to himself. Each time the nettles moved forwards, he pulled away his hand, maintaining the same distance between them. He stared at the nettles, fascinated.

At the end of the wall, the vegetation thinned out. The grass had been flattened and worn into a path which led over to a dark opening in one of the walls. A piece of sacking hung in the opening, and beyond it, three steps led down into an old cellar. Gavin looked round and then went over and tentatively pulled aside the sacking. He could see an old paraffin stove and some pans and spoons. He bent low and half tripped down the steps. The sacking fell into place again, plunging everything into a gloomy half-light. There was a strong smell of burnt wood, paraffin and dirt. Part of the floor was raised in one corner to make a crude sort of bunk. An old trench coat was spread across the bricks. As soon as Gavin saw it, he went across and lay down on the coat.

"My house," he whispered to himself. "My home."

He turned over on his side and for a few minutes dozed in a half-sleep. His breathing had slowed down because now there was nothing to be frightened of.

When he opened his eyes and they got accustomed to the darkness, he examined the cramped cell in which he lay. The roof was bricked like a barrel-vault. He reached out, but it was quite dry. Hanging on the opposite wall, there was an old glass-fronted picture of cows grazing by a meandering river. Sitting on a shelf beneath the picture were about twenty pairs of spectacles. Many were old-fashioned in design, but some were very up-to-date.

Suddenly there was someone outside the cellar. A pile of wood was dropped. A trouser leg appeared beneath the sacking.

Gavin sat up on the bunk. There was no fear.

"Have you brought them?" he asked.

"Yes. Not all, though," came back a thin tired voice.

"Where are the rest?"

"Can't bring them all, can we now?" The voice ended with a little chuckle.

"Were they trampled? Were they?!"

"No. No. Ah rescued them."

A little old man, sharp-featured and wizened, bent through the opening and pushed his way in. There was a white stubble about his face, but otherwise it was lined with dirt-filled cracks which looked even darker in the gloom. In his hand he held an old leather bag containing vegetables. On his nose rested two pairs of glasses, one on top of the other. He looked across at Gavin. There was no anger. "You passing through?"

Gavin caught sight of the vegetables. "Yer didn't bring them all?"

"No. Can't bring them all, can we now? Must be careful."

"Mustn't trample."

The little man looked round over his shoulder and smiled. "Ah didn't."

Gavin nodded and then watched as the little man took the vegetables out of the bag and laid them all on the ground by the paraffin stove. With a sigh, the little man stood up as straight as he could and surveyed the row of vegetables. "Carrots. It'll be carrots."

He flashed his little black eyes at Gavin. "Sorry. But Ah didn't get more. Only carrots. Sorry, sorry, sorry." Suddenly he turned on Gavin and his eyes burned. "Ah said … said it! Sorry! What are you shouting about? Sorry! Ah said it … said it…." His voice trailed away and his eyes became only those of a quiet old man again.

"Alright, Ah can get the rest, easy." Gavin spoke clearly. There was no fear.

Soon the carrots were simmering in an old battered pan. Gavin had watched the little man carefully as he prepared them. Beneath the pan, a little wood-fire burnt hot and smelled sweetly, smoke curling into the nettles. The little man sat on his hunkers, watching the bubbles rising in the clear water. He took a clean red handkerchief from the side pocket of his jacket and rubbed the side of his nose. "Soon be ready."

"You seen June?"

"It'll soon be ready. Ahh...." He smelled the pan and rubbed the palms of his hands against his greasy pinstripe trousers.

For a long time they both stared at the simmering pan in silence. Then Gavin spoke. "You seen June? When you picked them?"

"No, but Ah've got another pair. In May, Ah think. Look." He took an old pair of National Health spectacles from inside his jacket. "That makes twenty-three pairs. Twenty-three pairs ... never know when you'll need them, do you?" For a moment the little man stared at the new spectacles, completely absorbed.

"June's me girlfriend. She's coming here. We're going to live in this house."

"Alright, son. We'll wait for her. See, look, the carrots is ready. You got a bowl? Look, Ah'll lend you this one."

"You'd better put this one out for June. In case she comes."

"Aye. Right, then."

Gavin took the soup bowl in both his hands. It had a faded willow-pattern. He placed it on his knees and began spooning out and eating the soft carrots.

The little man smiled at Gavin. "You like that. You passing through then?"

"June might come here."

"Oh, Ah see."

"See, they might be following her ... no trampling...."

The little man began nodding to himself. "No, Ah was lucky. There they were. All those people walking over them. The glass was unbroken. Ah held them out. They never want them though. Never know when you'll need them, do you?"

"Never know. Nobody knows. Never know. Never," replied Gavin quietly.

"Some call us Owd Harry. They don't know whether Ah'm here

or not. Some of them believes Ah died years back. Not all though. Some of the kids see me, but they always run off. Bombsite Harry." He chuckled to himself. "Some of them believes Ah died years back."

"If June comes, she'll tell us what to do next."

"Oh aye, Ah expect she will. When you expecting her? Tomorrow or when?"

"Ah don't know. She might be a long time." Gavin paused. "But she shouldn't be long. You brought them, instead."

"Aye."

"Where are the others, then?"

"Twenty-three pairs Ah've got. Twenty-three pairs. Never knar when you need them, do you, son?"

Gavin put down his bowl.

"World record that," continued the little man. "Must go to the bank tomorrow and invest them all. Only way nowadays."

"My Dad won a prize. That's what Ah was going to do with mine. That's all Ah need … all Ah need … mustn't trample … must they?"

"Ah knar, son."

"They were all going to trample us. Ah saw them running. But Ah've got a job. Ah know. My country. They don't know."

"Ah knar, son. An' some of them believes Ah've been dead for years. Mind you, they don't come. Not nowadays, like."

Gavin leaned forward. "What did you do when it sucked them all up?"

"Invest them all, son. Invest them all. Foresight." He tapped a lens of the front pair of spectacles sitting on his nose.

"Did you see it?"

"Aye. 'Course Ah saw it. Flames and heat everywhere. Trapped, but Ah knew. Foresight." He tapped his spectacles again.

"Did you see her, then?"

Suddenly the little man became agitated. "Don't ask me about it, son. Don't ask me about it. She was moving … sort of twitching and shivering, and then … don't ask me about it now…."

"Why do yer…?"

The man put his hands to his ears and shook his head violently.

Gavin remained silent for some minutes. When he began speaking again, his words were clear and articulate. "One day Ah'll win too. This is my country. Ah know. You don't, do you?"

"Look, son, Ah think you ought to go. Ah've got a big list to make up before Ah go to bed. Catalogues and investments." He bent down and from underneath an old orange box pulled out an old-fashioned typewriter. Everything on it but the keys was covered in dirt and dust. "You go now, son. Ah'll show you the quickest way."

Gavin got up and nodded. The little man pushed through the sacking and led Gavin outside. The sun was still quite high and warm. The six o' clock hooter went at one of the factories. Gavin followed the little man through the maze of crumbling walls and piles of debris until they came to the edge of the buildings.

The man pointed up the hill, then touched his forehead with his hand. "Straight up the drive, sir. That's your quickest way."

With barely a nod, Gavin ran off and began scrambling up the hill. When he turned round, the little man had gone. The low walls of the buildings seemed all alike and there was no sign of the entrance to the cellar.

It took Gavin nearly a quarter of an hour to reach the top of the hill. There was a big field, gently rounded like a huge dome, so that the horizon in any direction was unbroken grass. Gavin ambled along, dragging his feet in the short grass. When he reached the highest point in the field he did not turn around to look behind. His eyes were fixed on a long fence and across another field to a row of ash and sycamore trees. There was nothing beyond the trees.

He ran down to the fence and quickly climbed over. On the other side, there was a farm track which curved away from the fence and led towards the row of trees. Gavin followed the deep and uneven tractor ruts, running from one side of the track to the other with a newly-found energy. When he reached the trees, he saw that there were other trees behind but at a lower level. The ground sloped away suddenly and the track ran off to the left. Gavin looked down through an opening in the trees and gradually his face softened and his eyes warmed.

Below the wood was the Jubilee Pit and beyond its surrounding waste-heaps, the new red-brick houses of the estate.

"Ah know! Ah know!" He laughed in his high-pitched laugh and began running down the steep path among the trees. "Ah know! Ah know! Ah know! They don't know! They don't know! They don't! They don't! They don't...!"

He was still shouting as he broke out from the trees and sped on to the cinder track. Here the path was wider and bordered a rough field, sometimes used as a football pitch. On his left were the buildings of the Jubilee pithead. The huge wheels were spinning round and the black cables were dancing in the sky. Behind the pithead was the row of pitman's cottages, but Gavin had eyes for neither. He ran straight on down the cinder track.

Soon he was becoming tired again, and his feet were heavier upon the ground. He slowed up and shouted between breaths. "June, you coming...? Come on! Ah know, man, Ah know!" He walked on, listening, but there was nothing but a low hum coming from the ventilation house. "She's got to... she's ... don't ask me about it ... don't ask me about.... June."

Ahead lay the barren area of slag. He half stumbled, half crawled up one of the hillocks of sliding shale. "June ... Ah know," he whispered to himself. "June ... nobody trampled.... You coming...? You coming...?" He slithered down the other side, ran down a deep gulley and scrambled up another hillock. At the top he listened for a while. There was the smell of burning sulphur in the air. He turned to look back at the mine and up the hill.

"Nobody ... nobody's coming ... you coming? Nobody's coming, no one. Ah didn't ... nobody's coming...." He was whimpering quietly and shaking a little. Then his body became slack and his limbs loosened. He took a step forward and the sliding grey rocks carried him smoothly to the bottom of the shaley bank.

He looked up. Thirty feet away from him was a large burning hole, and around it grass was growing. The grass was dried and green but unburned. A new light came into Gavin's face, his whimpering died away and his body tightened. He jumped and ran over to the side of the burning hole. The red-white cinders were there, the searing heat and the blue and yellow flames dancing and weaving inside. But he had no eyes for the inside of the hole and there was a little smile on his face that was growing. He was staring at the green grass on the other side.

"Billie," he whispered, "Billie."

Nearby there was another burning hole, but smaller. A flame leaped out of it, flickered, and caught his attention.

He spun around and cupped his hands. "Billie!" he shouted, but the soft cinder at the edge was crumbling. He looked up and shouted again. "Billie! Billie!"

He screamed and jabbed the hard ground with his foot, but the earth had decided. In a silent and swift movement, the whole edge of the hole collapsed and carried him down into the hellish red depths below. His piercing cry was lost in the moment a cloud of sparks rose into the sky.

A breath of wind bent the grass towards the new rim of the hole. A flame spurted out and licked around the brittle green stems, licked again and they suddenly became hot, but they did not light as the flame melted back into the red-white heat below.

Suddenly, three little boys appeared at the top of the shaley bank. They were all panting because they had all been running for some minutes. One was carrying a plastic rifle.

"Ah thought Ah heard a shout."

"Aye, but there's nee-one there, is there?"

"No," replied one of the boys.

"No. Then come on. Let's gerron with the game."

The group split up, leaving the boy with the plastic rifle at the top of the hillock. He lay down, put the rifle to his shoulder and trained the sights on one of his friends below.

## ACKNOWLEDGEMENTS

My deepest thanks to Ian Thorp of Archive Publishing, for his skills, support and enthusiastic commitment in producing this edition of *Well Below Average*.

I would also like to thank the sometime North East resident artist and engraver, Norman Wade, for providing the limited edition lithograph print, taken from my own collection, which forms the basis of the cover illustration. All attempts to contact Mr Wade or his estate and negotiate formal permission to use this lithograph have been unsuccessful. If Mr Wade or his representative is able to contact us we shall be very happy to appropriately acknowledge him in any future edition.

Finally, my sincerest thanks to Celia Gunn for her loving support and technical assistance in enabling my youthful creation to shine out into the wider world.

Anthony Thorley was an eighteen-year-old between school and university when he wrote *Well Below Average*, his only novel, in the early 1960s. Now, over forty years later, he is a retired consultant psychiatrist and medical policy adviser who lives in South West England and pursues an academic interest in indigenous traditions as found in legendary and sacred landscape, but still finds time to passionately follow the tortuous travails of his favourite football team, Newcastle United.

See www.earthskywalk.com and www.thealchemicaljourney.com for further details of his current activities.

Printed in the United Kingdom by
Lightning Source UK Ltd., Milton Keynes
142389UK00001B/45/P